Join the Lit~~~~amily
Five Generations of Pioneer Girls

Martha Morse, Laura's great-grandmother
born 1782
Martha was born to a wealthy landowning family in Scotland. She loved her family, but she also wanted to see the world, and one day she left her home to start a new life in America.

Charlotte Tucker, Laura's grandmother
born 1809
Martha's daughter Charlotte was born a city girl, and grew up near the bustling port of Boston. Charlotte had a restless spirit and traveled farther and farther west, before settling in Wisconsin.

Caroline Quiner, Laura's mother
born 1839
Charlotte's daughter Caroline spent her childhood in Wisconsin, and her days were busy helping her mother keep their little frontier farm running. Caroline grew up to be Ma Ingalls, Laura's mother.

Laura Ingalls
born 1867
Caroline's daughter Laura traveled by covered wagon across the frontier. When Laura grew up, she realized the ways of the pioneer were ending and wrote down the stories of her childhood in the Little House books.

Rose Wilder, Laura's daughter
born 1886
Laura's daughter, Rose, traveled from South Dakota to the Ozark Mountains of Missouri. She grew up hearing the stories of her mother's frontier girlhood and determined that one day she would be a new kind of pioneer.

Laura
and her mother, Caroline

Martha
(1782–1862)

Betsy	Louis	Linus	Lydia	Thomas	Charlotte
(b. 1800)	(b. 1802)	(b. 1803)	(b. 1805)	(b. 1807)	(1809–1884)

Martha	Joseph	Henry	Martha
(1832–1836)	(1834–1862)	(1835–1882)	(1837–1927)

Mary	Laura	*m.* Almanzo Wilder
(1865–1928)	(1867–1957)	(1857–1949)

Rose
(1886–1968)

The Little House
Family Tree

m.   Louis Tucker

m. Henry Quiner (1807–1844)	Caroline (b. 1811)	Mary (b. 1813)	Nancy (b. 1816)	George (1820–1821)

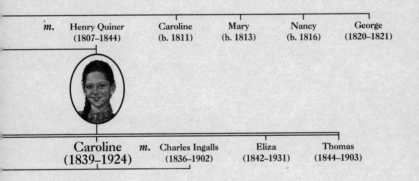

Caroline **(1839–1924)** *m.* Charles Ingalls (1836–1902)	Eliza (1842–1931)	Thomas (1844–1903)

Caroline (1870–1946)	Charles (1875–1876)	Grace (1877–1941)

Little Farm *in* the Ozarks

Roger Lea MacBride

Illustrated by David Gilleece

SCHOLASTIC INC.
New York Toronto London Auckland Sydney
Mexico City New Delhi Hong Kong

ISBN 0-439-15436-7

12 11 10 9 8 7 6 5 4 3 2 1

0 1 2 3 4 5/0

Printed in the U.S.A.

40

First Scholastic printing, January 2000

For my daughter Abby,
who shares with me the legacy of Rose.
In them both, God got it right.

Contents

Thief!   *1*

Peeping Frogs   *14*

Tree-Topping   *21*

Abe's Wolf Story   *33*

Fresh Greens   *41*

Market Day   *56*

Fighting Mules   *70*

The New Room   *90*

Chickens   *102*

Going Fishing   *111*

The Flood   *129*

Baby Birds   *143*

Visiting Alva   *155*

Off to School   *168*

New Girl   *175*

Afternoon Lessons   *191*

In Trouble   *206*

Summer   *223*

Picnic   *235*

Jungle of Green   *248*

Spelldown   *256*

Harvest Moon   *271*

Little Farm
in
the Ozarks

Thief!

Rose was sitting at the table in the little log house on Rocky Ridge Farm, finishing a letter to Grandma Ingalls, when she heard snarling outside in the dark, snowy woods. Fido, the little white terrier with black and tan spots, raised his head from the hearth and growled deep in his chest. His ears lay flat against his head.

"What was that?" Rose asked.

Mama closed her book and looked at Papa.

"That's a new one on me," he said. "Might be it's just a bobcat, but I'd best check the horses." He set down the leather horse collar he was oiling and wiped his hands on a rag.

Papa lit the lantern and pulled on his heavy buffalo coat. Fido followed him to the door. Papa took his gun down from its rack. "Stay here, boy," he told Fido. "I can handle this."

Mama laid more wood on the fire and hugged herself against the chill air that blew in when Papa opened the door.

Rose read the letter to herself by the light of the lamp:

"Dear Grandma," she had written. "Thank you very much for the good, warm socks, and for sending us the *De Smet News* every week. I am reading the story about poor General Custer.

"It is not so cold here as South Dakota, but my feet get cold sometimes. It snowed today. But Papa said spring will come soon, even if it is just Febuary! I like Missouri, but I miss everyone so very much. Your loving grand-daughter, Rose."

"Mama, how do you spell this month?"

"Feb-ru-ary," said Mama. "How does it sound?"

Rose saw her mistake and squeezed a small "r" in between the "b" and the "u."

They both looked up when they heard Papa open the outside door to the lean-to and kick the snow off his boots.

"Everything seems to be in order," he said. "The horses are quiet and I don't see any strange tracks in the snow."

Papa went back to oiling the collar.

"I was thinking, Bess," Papa said to Mama. "It's getting on toward spring and I'll be needing some help around the place. Reynolds at the general store told me this morning that here in the Ozarks folks plant their peas in February and their potatoes in March."

"I can scarcely believe it, Manly," Mama said. "We never planted anything before April in South Dakota. Are you sure he wasn't pulling the wool over your eyes?"

"I wouldn't have believed it myself," Papa said. "But Reynolds has his onion sets and seed potatoes in stock already, and he just put his plows and hoes out as well. Some fellows were in today signing their crop liens."

"What is the interest?" asked Mama.

"Fifteen percent," Papa replied.

"Why, that's as bold as thievery!" Mama complained. "How can we ever get ahead when we must wait four more years for the apple trees to bear fruit?"

"We've been through all that," Papa said calmly. "We have acres of good timber to hack into railroad ties and fence rails that we can always sell. But I can't do it alone and still raise our own corn and grain."

"I'm just not accustomed to waiting so long for a crop to come in," said Mama. "In South Dakota, we had the wheat crop to count on every summer."

Suddenly Fido barked. They all heard a burst of cackling.

"The henhouse!" Mama cried out. Rose's heart fluttered in her chest.

Papa and Mama jumped up at the same time. They threw on their coats and shoes. Papa grabbed his gun again. Mama lit the lantern and they both rushed out the door with Fido leading the way.

Rose shivered in the doorway and watched the lantern light throw trembling shadows among the trees as Mama and Papa ran. Then the light disappeared into the henhouse. She could hear their voices, but she could not tell what they had found.

Finally they came walking back. Someone else was with them! When they drew close, she was shocked to see it was a boy. Papa gripped him by the arm. The boy jerked his shoulder, trying to pull away. His hat fell to the ground and Mama picked it up. Rose backed into the house and they all came in.

"All right, son," Papa said in his most sober voice. "Now just you calm down a spell. Have a seat over there, by the table."

The boy sat down with a huff. He tucked his hands under his elbows and scowled. His thin, pale face poked out of clothing that looked like a pile of old rags. His coat was a man's threadbare suit jacket that hung to his knees. His pants were too big also, man's pants that had been cut off and patched. They were so big the pockets hung on the inside of his legs. His patched shirt was made of flour sacks, sewn with twine. The soles of his shoes flapped loose. A white feather clung to one of the pant legs. He glared at Rose and stuck his chin out defiantly.

Rose didn't know what to think. She had never seen such a stern look on Papa's face. Mama's face was grave and furrowed.

"Now, son," Papa said. "Let's have your name."

The boy stared at the floor in silence. Papa watched him, waiting and stroking his chin.

"We're going to straighten this out, one way or another," he said. "Stealing is serious business. We can go into town and talk to the sheriff if you like. Now why don't you tell us, who are your folks?"

"Ain't got none," the boy muttered in a raspy voice. He shivered and hugged himself.

"Come sit by the fire," Mama said. "You must be cold."

The boy got up and moved his chair over by the fireplace. He held his palms out to the flames and then rubbed them together. Rose sat on the big bed. She couldn't take her eyes off him. The boy looked about her age, which was eight, or perhaps a bit older. His face was plain. His ears stood out, and his nose was too big. His blue eyes seemed to show nothing at all. Rose noticed a bad smell had come into the house.

"Everybody has folks somewhere," Papa said. "Are you from these parts?"

"I ain't from nowhere," the boy said defiantly. Rose thought she saw his mouth wobble in the flickering firelight. Mama and Papa looked at each other over the boy's head.

"You must be living somewhere nearby, son," Papa said. His voice was softer now and his eyes shone with a gentle warmth. "If you're hungry we might be able to scare up a bite or two."

The boy looked at Papa for the first time.

"Are you hungry, son?"

The boy nodded. Papa let him sit warming in front of the fire while Mama put up some beans and cold potatoes in the spider-legged skillet to heat in the fireplace. The food began to sizzle and the room filled with the warm smell of cooking. Rose spotted a tear glittering on the boy's cheek.

"Now, just you relax. We aren't going to harm you," Papa said. "But you must tell us who you are. We can help, if you're alone."

"I ain't alone," the boy said. "I got my big brother. He's out a-working, is all."

"I'm Mr. Wilder," Papa said. "This is my wife, and our daughter, Rose."

"Hello," Rose said softly. The boy looked at her, but his face was blank, like a clock without hands. She could not tell what he was thinking.

"I'm Swiney," the boy finally said. "Swiney Baird. It's just me and my big brother, Abe."

"What about your folks, your ma and pa?"

"Dead," Swiney said simply.

He licked his lips and swallowed. His eyes followed Mama lifting the skillet out of the fireplace and spooning the steaming beans and potatoes onto a plate on the table.

"All right, Swiney," Mama said. "Come and eat."

Swiney pulled his chair over, sat down, and spooned the hot food into his mouth as fast as he could. Mama wrinkled her nose and frowned as she watched him. In an instant he was mopping up the plate with a piece of corn bread. Rose had never seen anyone eat so fast.

Mama took the empty plate away. Swiney stood up and looked around the little log house, as if to leave. But Papa motioned with his hand to sit back down.

"Now, then," Papa said. "Let's see if I have this right. Your folks have passed on, and you live with your brother. Where is that?"

Swiney pursed his mouth and stared into his lap. "Yonder," he said after a long pause, jerking his thumb. "On Kinnebrew's place. In the tenant house."

"Kinnebrew," Mama said slowly. "I've heard that name in town. Aren't they the folks who moved here from Illinois last fall?"

Swiney nodded his head.

"And your brother," Mama said. "He left you nothing to eat?"

"The latch busted on the door. Raccoons got in and stole every bit."

"But surely the Kinnebrews would take you in for a meal."

Swiney shook his head gravely. "Abe says they're city dudes. They don't like us country jakes." Then he looked at Mama, his eyes suddenly wide with fear. "You ain't a-going to tell them, is you? There wasn't no real harm in it, honest. I was just a-looking for eggs is all."

"Don't you worry about that," Papa said. "The important thing is that you don't have to steal from us to eat, Swiney. We'd never let a boy go hungry if we had a crumb to spare. Now, when is your brother coming home?"

"I ain't sure," said Swiney. He wiped his nose with the back of his dirty hand. His nails were chipped. "He drove a load of timber to Cabool."

"Cabool is a good two days' wagon trip," said Papa. "You must stay here with us tonight."

"But I cain't," Swiney whined, standing up. "I got to be going, mister."

"You'll stay here, son, and that's final," Papa said. "We'll fix a pallet for you to sleep on, by the fire, where it's warm. After a good breakfast we'll go to your place and see about fixing that latch."

Swiney's shoulders slumped and his face puckered as if to cry. But he sat quietly as Mama got out extra quilts and made up his bed.

When they were all settled for the night, Mama and Papa in their big bed and Rose in her trundle bed, Rose couldn't sleep. She listened to the crackling and hissing of the fire. She could hear Swiney tossing and turning under his covers. It frightened Rose to think a stranger would sneak into their henhouse and steal their eggs.

She did not think she liked Swiney very much. He was a thief, he was dirty, and he hadn't thanked Mama for his supper. But she was sorry he had no mother or father to make sure he had food to eat.

And it *was* something new to have a stranger in the house. Their first winter in Missouri had been lonely. Mama had kept Rose home from school until they could get a little money ahead. There were taxes to pay, and Rose needed new shoes.

Mama had said Rose could start school in July, when the next session began. By then the chickens would be laying again and Mama would have eggs to trade at Reynolds' store for necessities like new shoes and slate pencils.

"Besides, I have been a schoolteacher and I can certainly keep you up with your studies here at home," Mama had said.

It had been too cold, and the days too short, to explore outdoors or play with her friend Alva, who lived nearby on her father's farm. Her only other friends were Paul and George Cooley, who had come with Rose's family to Missouri from South Dakota. When they weren't in school, Paul and George helped their mama and papa run the Mansfield Hotel in town. Mr. and Mrs. Cooley were best friends with Mama and Papa. Rose saw Paul and George only on Sunday, when the two families went to their new church in town.

Thief!

Rose's restless thoughts were interrupted by Swiney crying out in his sleep, "Mumphster fluff!" Rose was curious about him. She wondered about his life, and how he got such a funny name.

Peeping Frogs

When Rose woke up in the chilly dawn, Mama was gathering up Swiney's bedclothes. Swiney was gone. He had slipped out of the house before the first rooster crow.

"Phew!" Mama said, making a face and holding the quilt away from her. "That boy smelled as skunky as an old dog. We might as well do a wash today, Rose."

"Why did he leave?" asked Rose.

"I expect he was afraid we would change our minds and turn him over to the sheriff," said Papa. "That little shaver's as bold as a sparrow. I'm sure last night wasn't the first time he found himself in a fix."

"Will he have to go to jail?"

Papa laughed. "Little boys don't go to jail for stealing eggs. There isn't a boy alive hasn't done something as bad or worse. He might be put in an orphanage, if we complained to the sheriff. But I wouldn't anyway. It's no crime to be hungry. I'll ride over to Kinnebrew's after breakfast and see how he's getting along."

The day dawned warm and soft. To look at the snow-covered ground was to be in winter. But when the sun rose high, its light fell strong on Rose's face. The sky was brighter than it had been in a long while. Before dinnertime the snow had turned mushy. In the bare spots the earth softened to reddish mud that clung to her shoes and made squishy, sucking noises when she walked.

While Rose helped Mama hang the sheets to dry in a sunny spot, she noticed a strange noise coming from the direction of Fry Creek. It sounded like a multitude of tiny bells, or many people whistling.

"I hear it, too," said Mama. "I wonder what it could be? It's too early for grasshoppers and crickets."

After dinner, when she was done with her laundry chores, Rose walked down toward the creek to explore. The whistling sound grew louder and louder. It seemed to be coming from a marshy place near the creek. But she couldn't see what was making such a racket. She walked toward the marshy spot. When she got close to it, when the sound was at its loudest all around her, it suddenly stopped.

Rose stood there for a long moment in confusion. There was nothing to see but swampy water full of dead leaves and the dead stems of last year's grass and reeds. Then she heard a single peep close by her. "*Peent*," something said. She stood very still, trying to see what had made that sound without startling it into silence. Farther away, there was an answer, "*Peent. Peent.*" In no time that whole swamp was alive with the noise of all those *peent*s.

Rose took a step. A fallen branch crackled under her foot. Immediately she saw several splashes in the water and the noise stopped again. She squatted down at the edge of the swamp and looked closely into it. All she could see at first was decaying leaves and bubbles and twigs.

Then she spotted some bubbles close together that seemed to move. She stared at those bubbles for the longest time, until finally she saw that they were a tiny pair of frog's eyes and a little frog's nose floating in the murky water. But as long as she sat there, no frogs would peep.

She walked a little way from the swamp and waited. In a minute, it started again. *"Peent. Peent. Peent."* But no matter how hard she tried to sneak up on the frogs, they would not peep when she was close. So she backed far away and just listened. It lightened her soul to hear those frogs singing their hearts out. Rose realized with astonishment that even though it was still winter, this was a sound of spring, the very first sound of spring.

Rose was telling Mama about the peeping frogs when Papa came riding home on May.

Behind him, riding together on a mule with notched ears, were a young man and Swiney.

"We have company," Mama said with a sigh, "and I can't think what we have to feed them. Draw a pail of water from the spring, Rose. At least we can make tea."

When Rose brought the water, Mama and Papa were talking to the young man, who held his battered hat in his hand. Swiney stood beside him, staring at the ground and kicking at a clump of snow.

"This is our daughter, Rose," Mama said. "Rose, this is Abe Baird, Swiney's big brother."

"Hello," Rose said politely.

"Pleased to make your acquaintance, Rose," Abe said in a warm, deep voice. His face was young and smooth, like a boy's. But it was also strong and bony, like a grown man's. A great shock of black hair fell across his forehead. His thick eyebrows met in the middle. Rose couldn't help staring at him. He didn't look anything like Swiney at all.

"It's like I was a-telling Mr. Wilder, ma'am," he said to Mama. "Swiney's and me's ma and pa passed on when Swiney was just a pup. Ma died birthing our baby sister. I reckon she was wore out after a-bringing twelve little ones into this world. The apoplexy carried off Pa just six months after."

"Twelve children," Mama said in wonderment. "However did you manage? Where are the rest?"

"We stuck together for a spell," Abe said. "But we durn near starved. In time all us kids just flew off like a bunch of quail. The little ones was a-taken in here and there. The older ones went out to find work. Swiney here always was a fractious little hornet, so I kept him on with me.

"But I ain't been much of a pa. I'm real sorry about last night. I told Swiney, stealing ain't no path to go."

He turned his head and spat a stream of amber tobacco juice onto the ground.

"Well, you must stay to supper," Papa said. Mama cleared her throat. "We haven't much," Papa went on. "But what we have . . ."

"I ain't a-aiming to put no burden on

you'uns," Abe said. "No sirree. I brung you some meat in this here poke, to show no harm meant." He reached into a sack at his feet and pulled out a dead raccoon by the tail. Rose had seen the skins of raccoons that her friend Alva had trapped.

"I don't think . . . " Mama began. "I mean, I wouldn't know the first thing about cooking a . . . what is it?"

"Coon, ma'am," said Abe. "You folks ain't tasted no coon yet?"

"No," Mama said firmly. "I'm not sure we're quite ready for that."

"Ain't nothing to it," Abe said heartily. "Why, coon's some of the best eating meat we got in these here hills. Swiney and I'll skin it, and I can tell you just how to cook it."

Mama looked at Papa. The color drained from her face. But there was nothing more she could politely say. Abe would not take no for an answer, and Mama would never argue against the generosity of strangers.

Tree-Topping

Abe and Swiney stayed to supper of roast raccoon and turnips. After they had ridden away on their mule, Mama scraped her full plate onto a slab of wood and put it outside for Fido.

"I just couldn't eat it," she said, making a face. "I have never seen so much greasy fat on an animal."

"I liked it," Rose said. "It tasted like rabbit."

"I wouldn't have guessed it myself, but it was delicious, Bess," agreed Papa.

"It did smell good," Mama admitted with a chuckle. "But that's the last time you are go-

21

ing to find a raccoon in my oven."

"It won't be the last we see of Abe and Swiney," Papa said. "Abe is going to be our hired man."

"Are you sure he's reliable?" asked Mama. "Isn't he sharecropping for Mr. Kinnebrew?"

"He is," Papa said. "But he's also cutting railroad ties and fence rails on his own. He's a good strong boy, just a little young and rough around the edges is all. And Swiney can help with the chores around the place."

"Very well," Mama said. "You can never tell through what door Providence may walk."

After breakfast the next morning Abe and Swiney came back.

"You listen to Mrs. Wilder same as if she was our ma," Abe told Swiney before going off with Papa to the woodlot.

"Now, Swiney," Mama said. "First thing we need to do is get you a good hot bath."

"A bath?" Swiney said in a whining voice. "But why? Abe don't make me take no bath."

"I'm not Abe," Mama said, "and you've got skunk scent in all your clothes. Don't you smell it?"

"No, ma'am," said Swiney, wrinkling his big nose. "I did catch me a skunk a little time back. But I cain't smell nothing now."

Rose giggled. Swiney glared at her.

"So long as you are going to be part of this family, I'll thank you to leave skunk business to the skunks," said Mama.

"Awww," Swiney grumbled.

But he took his bath anyway, in a corner of the house behind a sheet Mama had hung from the rafters. While he splashed around in the tin tub, Rose helped build a fire under the big cast-iron pot outside. Then Mama scrubbed his threadbare clothes with soft soap. She gave him Rose's extra flannel union suit to wear while he sat in a chair and his things dried, hanging from the fireplace mantel.

When he was dressed again, Swiney still looked shabby, but his face shone pink and clean, and his dark hair glistened. Then Mama said Rose could show him around the farm.

The weather had turned wintry again. Silver-gray clouds pressed down upon the hills. A pair of jaybirds, crying out in shrill voices, flashed across the open space in front of the house to hide in a bush. Rose shivered against the cold and pulled her woolen fascinator tight around her head.

The surface of the snow had frozen to a crust as hard as a plate. The horses' hooves had left holes in the mud, which had frozen into little pools of ice. The ice crackled when they walked on it.

Rose kept her thoughts to herself as they walked by the henhouse. Swiney stared at the ground until they had passed it.

Then Rose showed Swiney the new barn that their neighbors had helped Papa build one day in the fall. They looked at the mares, Pet and May, in their stalls. They were fat and sleek from having so little work to do in the winter.

Then they fed handfuls of oats to the colts, Little Pet and Prince. Papa had been breaking and gentling them all winter. Soon they would be old enough to sell. Rose hated to think of it. But she knew they couldn't keep the colts forever, and someday the mares would have new ones.

Swiney hardly spoke a word as Rose told him about their long trip to Missouri from South Dakota in the wagon. She told him about her friend Alva, and how she sometimes went with Alva in the darkness before dawn to check Alva's trap lines for rabbits and raccoons.

Swiney threw rocks at squirrels and the little black-capped chickadees that flitted from branch to branch singing, "Day-day-day."

It was wicked to hurt or kill anything that one didn't need. But Rose did not know Swiney well enough to scold him.

Swiney pulled out a folding knife and began to sharpen it by scraping it on a whetstone he carried in his pocket. He spit on his arm and shaved off a tiny patch of the fine, damp hair.

"Why did you do that?" Rose asked.

"To see if it's right sharp," Swiney said. "That's how to tell."

"Can I try it?"

"Girls ain't supposed to play with knives," Swiney scoffed. "Besides, this here was my pa's knife. Abe gave it me and I ain't never let nobody else touch it." He wiped the blade on his pants, snapped it shut, and dropped it back in his pocket.

They walked to the apple orchard. Fido sniffed for rabbits around the brush piles left from Papa's clearing the land. Papa had felled forest trees all winter. As soon as the ground had thawed enough, he would replant all of the slender young apple saplings that came with Rocky Ridge Farm when they first moved there in the fall.

"When I am thirteen years old, all those trees will bear apples," Rose explained. "Then the apples will go on the trains to big cities, where people will buy them to bake pies."

Then, Rose added to herself, Mama and Papa will have everything they ever wanted. Those fragile young apple trees were their whole future. Mama and Papa had brought Rose here from South Dakota to get away from a drought. For as long as Rose had been alive, too little rain had fallen on the prairie and the wheat crop failed year after year. Finally they could live there no longer.

So they had packed all their belongings into

a little black wagon and driven to Missouri, to The Land of the Big Red Apple, with the Cooleys. They were starting a new life in a place where good water pours right out of the ground all year long and the winters are short.

The Land of the Big Red Apple was a name the railroad companies gave the Ozark Mountains, to persuade people to come there, buy land, and grow apples to ship on the trains.

Mama and Papa had come to Missouri to make a new future. They bought the little run-down farm, called it Rocky Ridge, and began to fix it up. They had been very lucky. The farm came with nearly a thousand apple saplings all heeled in, waiting to be planted. In a few years those apple trees would begin to bear fruit that Mama and Papa could sell. They would never want for anything again.

But for now, Rose knew they must make do with what they had.

Rose and Swiney were walking through the woods around the apple orchard when Swiney suddenly stopped and peered up at a particular tree.

"Want to play tree-topping?" he asked.

"What is that?"

"You ain't never tree-topped?" Swiney said, his eyes wide with amazement. "Just you watch."

Swiney climbed up the tree as quick as a squirrel. When he got near the top, it began to bend under his weight. He grabbed hold of a thin branch over his head. He let his legs swing out. Slowly, with a little groan, the tree bent down until Swiney's feet touched the ground.

Then he began to jump up and down, still holding the top of the little tree. Each time he came back down he bounced a little higher. The tree limbs rattled and shook wildly. Finally he bounced so high that the tree stood straight up and then bent all the way down on the other side until his feet touched the ground. Swiney had ridden that tree all the way over the top!

Rose had never seen anything like it. Swiney bounced way up in the air and then down the other side of the tree, back and forth, back and forth. Fido raced around the tree, barking excitedly. Rose shrieked with delight.

"Let me try!" she shouted.

Swiney stopped bouncing, but he held on to the branch. "Come and grab on," he said. Rose took it and held on as tight as she could. She felt the springiness in it.

"Now start a-jumping, is all," Swiney said. "Don't let go."

Rose took a little jump, but her feet barely left the ground.

"Come on," Swiney said. "Jump high, and keep a-jumping, high as you can."

Rose jumped higher and higher. She felt herself starting to fly. She laughed.

"Higher!" Swiney shouted. "Higher!" Each time she came down she saw his grinning face looking up at her, and then up she went again, higher and higher. But she still wasn't over the top.

Finally she pushed off with all her might, and she knew she was going to go over. She felt herself going up and up, as if she would never come down. Up and up, into the sky.

Just as she felt her feet swinging out from under her, she heard a sickening crack, like a gunshot. The branch she was holding didn't feel springy anymore.

Now she really *was* flying, spinning sickeningly, away from the tree. Then she was falling and falling, for the longest time. She heard herself crashing against branches as they flew by. She felt twigs whip her face and legs.

In an instant, everything came to a stop with a horrible thud that stole her breath. Lights exploded in her head. The back of her neck hurt. The side of her face burned. Her ears rang. Tears stung her eyes.

Rose tried to get up, but she could not move her arms and legs. She was in a peculiar, misty place of no sound, no time, and no color. There was only a warm stinging in her face, and the ringing in her ears, like bumblebees trapped in a jug.

Faintly, through the buzzing, Rose heard Swiney calling her name.

"Wha-what happened?" Rose asked in a quavering voice.

"That old tree broke right off," said Swiney. "You sure went a-flying."

Rose slowly got up, brushing off her coat. Her legs wobbled at first, but then she felt like herself again and laughed.

"That was fun," she said. "I want to do it again. I mean, without it breaking."

Swiney picked another tree. He bent it extra hard to be sure it wouldn't break. Then they took turns tree-topping. Rose lost her grip at first and tumbled to the ground. But soon she understood how to do it and she was flying again, watching the forest floor zoom away as she went up and up. Then she watched it come rushing at her as she came back down on the other side, Fido's pointy little face barking at her. Rose thought nothing could ever be so much fun.

Finally they were tired of tree-topping and walked quietly back to the house.

Rose still did not know if she liked Swiney. He was rough, and she could not forget that he had tried to steal from them. But they had had fun playing together.

"What on earth have you been up to?" Mama exclaimed when they got back. "Your face is scratched, your braids are all undone, and your coat! It's torn."

"I was running. And . . . and I fell," Rose fibbed. She didn't want to tell Mama about tree-topping. She was afraid Mama might forbid her to do it again. She *had* been running, and she *did* fall. Rose stole a sideways glance at Swiney. He was grinning at her. Rose struggled to keep her face straight.

"You were just running and fell?" Mama asked. She wiped her hands on her apron and raised an eyebrow doubtfully. She looked at Swiney and then back at Rose. "That's a mighty lot of scratches for running and falling. And look at that tear. It will need mending."

Rose held her breath. She was just about to tell Mama the truth when Mama sighed. "All right, then," she said. "Come sit while I dab some coal oil on those scratches. Then you two wildcats can gather some firewood. Abe shot two rabbits today. He and Swiney are staying to supper."

Abe's Wolf Story

Rose loved company. The little house rang with the warm sounds of rattling plates and lively voices. The everyday fire in the hearth seemed festive, and the everyday food tasted as good as Sunday's.

Rose especially liked Abe. She enjoyed the full sound of his deep voice, and his curious way of speaking.

"Yes, ma'am," he answered to a question of Mama's. "Our pa, he had no care but to build him a cabin and get his meat from the bounty of the forest. From day's ending to day's ending he was a-relying on the Providence of God. But Pa, he's gone to his reward, and poor Ma also, and them times are buried with them. It's the peaceful way of living that is past and gone."

"The whole country is pretty well settled up," Papa said, nodding. "Even on the open prairie, where we used to live, the game is mostly hunted out."

"When I was a little girl, the wolves would sometimes come at night and serenade our little house," said Mama.

"There's still wolves a-roaming these here hills," Abe said. "You don't see but a few now and then, but they are surely about. I recollect Pa a-telling wolf stories such as would put your hair straight up."

"Tell us one!" Rose blurted before she could stop herself. Abe laughed a great hearty laugh. Even Mama chuckled. She did not mind that Rose had spoken out of turn.

"Yes, Abe," Mama said. "We do so like to hear stories. I'm afraid Rose has heard nearly all of mine."

"Let me study on it a spell," Abe said, pursing his lips in thought. The whole house seemed to listen as they waited. The lamp purred peacefully on the table. Far away they heard the mournful whistle of a train. The coals in the fireplace settled with a crunching sound.

"Now this here's a story Pa told me when I was a sprout. I never could forget it," Abe began. "Pa, he was a fiddler. Now and again he'd fiddle here and there, at a frolic or a wedding. There always was music about him, a-singing or a-fiddling."

"My pa played the fiddle also," Mama said, her face shining in the warm light. "I think sometimes we never could have gotten through the hard times without his music. I miss it still."

"I am surely glad to hear of it," said Abe. "Pa left me his fiddle, you see, and I fiddle myself.

"Well, Pa was on his way home from a-fiddling one night. It was dark as a poke full of black cats. He'd left his gun home, a-thinking it weren't a far piece to walk and him a-having his hands full with the fiddle and all. But when he'd gone down the road a lick, he heard a terrible howl a-coming up the hollow at his back.

"Pa weren't afraid of much, but that howl put spring in his step. He knowed it were a wolf, and where there's one wolf, there's surely a pack. Soon enough, he heard more howling."

Abe got up and walked to the fireplace. He stood with his back to the fire, warming his hands behind him.

"Now Pa recollected there was an old empty house in the woods nearby, so he lit a shuck for it. He could hear them wolves a-crashing through the woods, a-getting mighty close. By the time he broke out into the clearing, he could hear them a-breathing on his heels.

"Them folks he was a-fiddlin' for that night had given him a poke full of leftover corn pone, so he throwed it on the ground, a-hoping them wolves would hold up to eat it.

"Pa ran into that empty house, a-thinking he were finally saved. He weren't too pleased to find the door busted clean off, and it being too dark inside to find a chunk of wood to block it up. He did find a ladder up to the loft, so he climbed it, quick as a squirrel and none too soon at that. The wolves come a-pouring into the house."

Rose's skin tingled with excitement. Everyone was very still, even Swiney, listening to Abe's every word. The only sound was the clock, clearing its throat to chime the hour.

"Them wolves—there must of been four or five—was bold with hunger, being they was in a pack and all. They was a-licking their chops, and a-snarling down there on the floor, and a-looking for a way to get up into that there loft.

"Pa figured he'd make out fine just a-setting up there. But then the biggest of them wolves, the leader of the pack, stood up, a-putting his paws on the wall. Then he jumped, and got his front paws hooked on one of them rafters. He slipped off, but them other wolves got the idea and the whole pack was a-jumping.

"Pa felt around in the loft and found himself a stick of wood. He started a-swinging it at them wolves, and a-kicking with his feet, a-knocking this one back, and that one. But he could see it was a losing fight. Them wolves weren't a-giving up.

"Pa was a-swinging that stick when once he missed and busted a place clean through the roof shingles where they was rotted. He got the idea he might fare better on the roof. So he broke him that hole bigger, grabbed his fiddle, and slung it by the cord over his back.

"He was a-pulling himself up through the hole, them wolves a-scratching and a-snarling just a few feet below, when the fiddle got snagged on the strings. He pushed and that there fiddle let out with an awful screech. Pa eased himself back down, and tried again. *Screech!* that old fiddle cried out.

"All of a sudden, Pa noticed them wolves was a-getting real peaceful like. He quick pushed the fiddle through the hole and climbed out onto the roof.

"Now he studied on his fix a spell and got himself an idea. He took up his bow and scratched himself a long note on the fiddle. Then he listened. It was quiet down below. So he started a-playing a slow tune. Them wolves either liked it, or it scared them. But they was real quiet, like they was a-listening. He looked down through the hole and them wolves was a-sitting there like a church full of mourners.

"So Pa kept right on a-playing, one tune after another. He played slow, then fast; loud, then soft. If he stopped, them wolves would stay still a spell, then they got restless and started a-snarling and a-jumping again.

"Some songs set them a-howling, low and sorrowful. Sometimes they just sat there polite as can be.

"It was a long night, but Pa played and played, a-laughing at them wolves. Finally the first light came a-creeping into the clearing. The big wolf slunk off into the forest. Then, one by one, the rest of them gave up and slipped away. Pa waited a good long while till it was sunup, and then he climbed down and walked on home."

Rose clapped her hands with delight when he was done. She loved scary wolf stories. "Tell another, Abe!" she cried out. "Please."

"That was a wonderful story, Abe," Mama

said, getting up to wind the clock. "But I think that's enough for tonight, Rose. We don't want to tire Abe out."

Rose was sorry to see Abe and Swiney leave. But it had been a wonderful evening. It left her eager to meet the next day, and all the days that would follow. It was a feeling, like the peeping frogs and the lengthening days, of newness and change. Rose felt it rushing through her veins. The rustle of spring was everywhere, even in Abe's voice.

Fresh Greens

Gentle spring rains fell all the next week, slowly melting the snow. Gray mist often hung in the air, or gathered in little wisps of clouds that settled in the valleys. The rain and gathering warmth began to soften the earth.

Abe did not come every morning. Sometimes he had spring chores to do for Mr. Kinnebrew. On those days Swiney stayed with Abe.

One day Papa hitched the mares and began to plow the new ground he had cleared for the garden, the orchard, and the crops. But almost as soon as he started, Papa came back to the house with a frown on his face. His shoes were balls of mud, and his overalls were spattered with it.

Mama and Rose were scrubbing the floor, so Papa stood in the lean-to.

"This beats all," he said. "It's as if the bottom dropped out of the earth! Nothing but mud. You could walk the whole forty acres and your feet never leave the ground. And the worst of it is, the horses' hooves sink right into it. They hurt themselves trying to pull out."

"Surely you can wait a bit, until the ground dries some," Mama said.

"I can but I shouldn't," said Papa. "There's too much plowing and logging to be done. We'll have to trade the colts for a pair of mules. They work better, and they have narrow feet that won't hurt the garden or get stuck in the mud.

"Spence at the livery stable was just saying the other day that he could use a good pair of young horses, to pull the buggies he hires out."

Rose sighed heavily. A hard lump jumped into her throat.

"But surely a pair of colts are not worth two full-grown mules," said Mama. "How will we make up the difference?"

"Spence knows my way with horses," Papa said. "He has been asking me to break some colts for him. I bet I can talk him into letting me work off the difference."

"It was bound to come to this sooner or later," said Mama. "We had to borrow Mr. Stubbins' mules last fall, to plow the ground for the garden. The colts are broken now, and there's no sense wearing out the poor mares."

So Papa put leads on Little Pet and Prince and walked them away from Rocky Ridge Farm, to a new life at the livery stable in town. They tossed their graceful heads and whinnied to their mothers as they went. Pet and May answered from the barn with troubled neighs. Papa had locked them in so they couldn't follow.

Rose could not stifle a sob as she watched them go.

"You mustn't cry," said Mama, hugging Rose to her. "There is no work for the colts here anyway. They will be happier pulling a buggy and getting some exercise."

But Rose could not make herself feel better. She remembered how the little colts had trotted alongside their mothers all that hard, dusty trip from South Dakota. She remembered how Prince would nuzzle her arm asking for a carrot or a bunch of clover. She remembered the time Papa had let her sit on Little Pet as he led the colt around the barn. Now she would never ride him again.

Rose went to the barn and stroked Pet's nose, and then May's. But they were fidgety. They kept sticking their heads out of their stalls into the hallway, looking this way and that for their colts. Across the open hallway the still-warm stalls stood empty and silent.

When Papa came back with the mules and put them in the barn, Rose did not go to look at them. The mules were not beautiful and graceful like horses. Mules were bred for work, not for riding. They didn't toss their heads gaily, like horses. Their necks were short and thick and their bellies low-slung. Their coarse coats did not shine, their ears were too big, and their mossy faces looked at everything with discontented eyes.

The next day Papa hitched up the mules and plowed the garden. He had broken the ground in the fall and hurt himself when the plow point struck a root. Now he knew to be very careful not to stumble. The ground was still full of roots, and rocks, too. The mules had to fight every inch of the way. The soil was as sticky as pudding. Everywhere Rose walked there was reddish-brown mud.

The new ground Papa had cleared was all stumps and piles of dead brush, surrounded by the bare trees. The world was brown and gray and muddy. Rose thought the farm looked as desolate as a cornfield after the harvest, bristly broken stalks.

When Papa finished plowing the garden, Mama and Rose went to work, clearing the rocks and hoeing it smooth. Pools of water stood in the holes where Papa had taken out stumps. For days and days they picked stones out of the mud, and Swiney came to help.

Swiney made a game of it, hurling stones at tree trunks and squirrels until Mama scolded him. But picking up those rocks was no game for Rose. The mud got on her clothes and under her nails. Her back ached from stooping over, and her hands became raw and chapped.

"Where did all these stones come from?" Rose asked with a weary sigh. They had picked stones out of the garden in the fall until the soil was clean. But now it was full of them again.

"I don't know," said Mama, pushing her hair from her face. Her cheek was streaked with mud. "The earth here is very thin. It just seems to grow them."

The days were often cold and damp. But it felt good to be out of doors after being cooped up all winter like a possum in its den.

The melting snow told the story of winter in the woods. On the forest floor she found skeletons of animals and scatterings of feathers where an owl or hawk had eaten a bird. Tiny nests told where mice had raised their litters.

On neighboring farms she could hear newborn calves bawling for their mothers. Flights of geese, crying joyfully in their harsh voices, circled the valley at sunset and landed in last year's fields to look for forgotten kernels of corn. Groundhogs sunned themselves on rocks, or waddled through the fields to feed along the streams.

Shyly at first, then more boldly, the forest birds rehearsed their spring voices. The simple chipping and aimless twittering that Rose had heard all winter gave way to new songs, clear and sweet and hopeful. "Cheerio! Cheerio! Cheerio!" the robins sang. Brilliant red cardinals cried, "What cheer! What cheer! What cheer!" Little white-throated sparrows called out, "Old Tom Peabody, Peabody, Peabody."

Rose whistled those songs as she worked. All the woods seemed to be a bustle of mysterious affairs.

Rose was resting from picking up rocks and throwing them to the side of the garden when she saw someone coming through the trees. At first she did not know who it was. But then she saw it was a little girl with fiery red hair sticking out from under her bonnet.

"Alva!" Rose cried out. It was her first friend in the Ozarks, Alva Stubbins. She had not seen Alva since before Christmas.

"Hello, Rose," Alva said. "Hello, Mrs. Wilder."

"Hello, Alva," Mama said. "What a pleasant surprise. What brings you visiting?"

"My ma sent me over with some sassafras," Alva said.

Alva handed Mama a bundle of small tree roots tied up with a string. Rose could smell the pungent odor from where she was standing.

"That's very nice," Mama said. "But I don't know what to do with it."

"It makes tea," Swiney piped up. "To thin your blood. Everybody takes sassafras tea in the spring."

Alva frowned at Swiney. "Yes," she said. "It perks your blood up when it gets too thick in winter."

"This is Swiney Baird," Rose said. "His big brother Abe is my papa's new hired man."

Alva looked at Swiney, but she did not say anything.

"Can Rose come and play a spell?" Alva asked Mama. "I found some pokeweed down by Wolf Creek. We could pick you a mess for salad."

"Pokeweed?" said Mama.

"It's greens," Swiney piped up again. "And cow parsley. We always eat greens in spring."

"I don't see why not," said Mama. "Are you sure you know what's good to eat, and what isn't?"

"Yes, ma'am," Alva said. "I help my ma with the picking every year. We ain't never got sick yet."

Rose took a pail from the house and walked down to Wolf Creek with Alva. Swiney trailed behind. Rose told Alva about the wonderful wolf story Abe had told at supper one night.

All through the story, Swiney kept interrupting to tell parts of it. Just as she was about to tell the ending, about Swiney and Abe's father playing the fiddle all night, Swiney shouted it out.

Then Rose frowned at Swiney, too.

At Wolf Creek, Alva showed Rose a clump of pokeweed. Rose had seen green leaves pushing up here and there in the forest, but she didn't know which ones she could safely eat.

"You take the little soft leaves," Alva explained. "But not the root. That's the bad part."

"I got a knife, so I'll be the cutter," Swiney announced. He took out his knife and started sharpening it.

"Who says?" said Alva. "We don't need no cutter anyway. We can just tear them off."

"Can not!" Swiney shouted. Rose was surprised at how foolish Swiney was being.

"Can too!" Alva shouted back. "You can just go find your own poke and cut it if you like. We don't care."

"Humph!" Swiney grumbled, shaving a little patch of arm hair. Then he began carving his name in the trunk of a tree.

Alva showed Rose how to check to make sure there weren't any bugs or insect eggs hiding on the undersides of the bright green leaves. They tore the tenderest leaves off and dropped them in the pail. Then Alva showed her lamb's-quarter and cow parsley. On the edge of the creek, growing right out of the clear cold water, they found watercress. "Try it," said Alva. "It's real good."

Rose pulled some of the tiny leaves from the stem and put them in her mouth. Nothing had ever tasted so fresh and tangy, like radishes. Rose had not realized how hungry she was for fresh vegetables. Swiney brought some poke-weed to put in the pail, but after a while he stopped helping.

Alva and Rose were busy picking when Swiney called out to them: "Watch me! Look! Bet you can't do this!" he shouted. He was standing next to a fence. He climbed up and began to walk shakily along the top rail, holding his arms out for balance.

"That's nothing. We don't care, anyway," Alva sniffed. Just as Swiney got to the end of the section, he tried to turn around. But he lost his balance. He fell, head first. Rose gasped. But just in the instant before Swiney's head would have hit the ground, one of his pant legs got tangled in the fence. He stopped short, hanging upside down, just above the ground.

"Ow!" he screamed. "I'm stuck!" He wriggled and tried to lift himself back up with his arms. He twisted and turned, and huffed and kicked. But try as he might, he couldn't unstick himself. His face turned bright red and the veins stood out on his neck.

"Ha, ha, ha," Alva shouted gleefully. "Now I know why they call you Swiney. You got your snout into everything. Now you look like an old hog at butchering time. Maybe we ought to take your knife and cut you up for sausage."

Rose giggled. She hadn't thought of it before, but Swiney really did get into things like a rooting hog.

"Get me down," Swiney pleaded. "Help me!"

"Maybe we ought to just leave him there," Alva said, putting her hands on her hips. "It would serve him right, sticking his swiney snout into everything. Whiney Swiney!" she shouted in singsong.

"No," Rose said. She didn't like Swiney as well as she liked Alva, and she could laugh at how foolish he looked. But Rose could never be truly mean, and especially not to poor Swiney, who had no mother or father. His face puckered up.

"Come and help," she said to Alva. Together they lifted Swiney up until his pant leg came loose. Then he fell to the ground in a heap, like a pile of old clothes.

Swiney got up and brushed himself off. His face was crimson, and pinched with anger.

"I guess you're really something," Alva said mockingly.

"Are you all right?" asked Rose.

"Awww, never mind!" Swiney shouted. He stomped off toward the house, and they followed him.

When the bucket was full of greens, Alva

53

went home. Mama cut the sassafras roots into short pieces and put them in a big kettle of water to simmer. The house quickly filled with a strong, spicy smell.

Then Rose brought pails of fresh spring water and helped Mama wash the greens, three times to be sure they were good and clean. Mama parboiled the greens in a pot. Then she drained off the water and added them to the salt pork that was frying in the skillet.

When everything was cooked, they sat down to eat it with chunks of fresh corn bread to sop up the delicious pot liquor. The greens were a little bit bitter, but it was a refreshing kind of bitter for tongues tired of beans, salt pork, and corn bread three times a day, six days a week.

Then Mama served them the sassafras tea, sweetened with molasses. It was tart and spicy and sweet, all at the same time. Rose liked it better than grown-up tea.

"That was delicious," Papa said, wiping his mustache with his napkin. "Sure whets a fellow's appetite for real garden food. I'd say it's about time to start planting."

"Yes, the garden is about ready and it's coming up on a full moon," said Mama. "After that will be time to put in the ground crops. Rose and I will go with you tomorrow to town and I'll pick up some onion sets and seed potatoes. And some seed to start my hotbeds."

Rose had hardly been to town since they first moved to Mansfield, only to church on Sunday when everything and everyone was quiet and sober. Each day on Rocky Ridge she heard the trains whistle as they arrived and left the station. She watched their ribbons of smoke unfurl above the trees and hills. She heard the school bell ringing and imagined all those children running not to be late for their lessons.

But she had never gone to town with Papa on his errands. Now she looked forward to seeing the town on a market day, full of life. It would be fun to see something different for a change.

Market Day

The next morning's chores were all done in a rush. Rose was in such a hurry, she spilled the water Mama had warmed for the chickens. It didn't do for them to drink water cold right from the spring, but Mama said there wasn't time to heat more. The hens would have to make do.

Rose scrubbed her face, hands, and feet in the washbasin in the lean-to. Mama washed where she had missed, the back of her neck and in her ears.

Then she brushed Rose's hair and plaited it tightly into two braids. When she was done she tied on Rose's yellow hair ribbons. Rose wriggled into her blue calico school dress. When she put her arm into the tight shoulders, she heard a ripping sound.

Rose looked at Mama and made a face.

"Never mind," Mama said. "I had hoped it would last till summer. We'll just have to get some goods today for a new one. No one will notice with your coat on."

Then Mama and Papa washed and dressed themselves. Mama put on her second-best dress, a calico that beautifully set off her long, shimmering, roan-brown hair. Then she wove her hair into one wide braid and wound it, lady-like, into a bun.

Papa combed bay rum through his hair. The rich scent always made going somewhere seem special. He put on a fresh pair of overalls, his jacket, and his felt hat. Mama and Rose tied on their bonnets. Then they were ready to go.

Mama and Rose carried their shoes to the wagon so they wouldn't get soiled.

Pet and May stamped their feet impatiently. Papa had brushed them so their coats shone brightly in the early light.

Patches of thin mist floated above Wolf Creek as they splashed across the ford to the other side. Then the wagon rumbled alongside it, through the little valley that lay between Rocky Ridge Farm and Mansfield. The creek chuckled to itself. The horses' hooves clattered on the flinty stones. The strong sun lay like a weight on Rose's shoulders. She wanted to take off her coat, but then she remembered the ripped shoulder of her dress.

A pair of crows flapped past them, diving and twisting playfully in the bliss of spring. A tufted titmouse called out from a bush as they passed, "Wheedle! Wheedle! Wheedle!" never stopping to catch its breath.

"Do you think Reynolds will give us credit enough to get all our spring provisions?" Mama asked over Rose's head.

"Can't see why not," said Papa. "Folks know me now, from my winter job, delivering coal oil for Mr. Waters. And I've sold our stove wood to half the houses in town. Anyone can see we're honest, hardworking farmers."

"It just makes me uneasy, Manly," said Mama. "It was hard enough on the prairie, praying all summer for the wheat harvest to come in only to see it blown away by cyclone, or burned up by drought.

"At least the prairie gave us free grassland to feed the livestock. Now with taxes and the mortgage, and this land so thin and stony, it's a wonder we can raise enough just to—"

"Now, Bess, you're putting the oak before the acorn," Papa interrupted. "Besides, you forget all that timber we have to be made into fence rails and railroad ties. Nothing can take that away. It's cash money we can always count on.

"And the hens will be laying again soon. We've always made out somehow. We always will." He smiled and reached over to squeeze Mama's hand.

Mama sighed and looked out across an orchard of grown apple trees they were passing. Rose prayed that their orchard would hurry and grow.

The bumpy, muddy wagon tracks turned

away from the creek and climbed a steep hill. The railroad tracks curved toward them and then ran alongside. When they crested the ridge, they could see the whole town spread out before them. The horses began to trot down the long, gentle hill into the center of town. Papa had to rein them in to keep their hooves from kicking up clods of mud.

Town was crowded. Farmers streamed in from all directions. The square swarmed with wagons and horses. Children raced shouting and laughing across the steaming muddy streets. Papa had to drive around the square twice to find an empty hitching spot.

Some men waved and called out to Papa, "Howdy, Wilder!"

While Papa hitched the team, Mama and Rose brushed off their feet and put on their stockings and shoes. Then they all walked on the gravel path around the square. Mama put her hand through Papa's arm, and held her skirt up from the muddy ground with the other. Rose thought Mama and Papa looked lovely together, walking like that.

Rose's senses were keen in the strong sunlight. It was exciting to be among all those people, to hear all the strange voices calling to each other. The loneliness of the cold, gray winter melted away.

In the middle of the square was a park, with trees and a bandstand. Around the square were the stores that all those people had come to trade in. The signs read "Newton's Groceries," "Coday's Drugs," "The Bank of Mansfield," "Opera House," and "The Mansfield Hotel," where Paul and George lived. The railroad tracks made one side of the square, with the depot for the Kansas City, Fort Scott, and Memphis Railroad. Some men were unloading boxes onto the platform with bumping sounds.

"Mama, can we visit the Cooleys? Please?" Rose pleaded.

"No," said Mama. "A hotel is a business. It is not a place for visiting."

Now they came to Reynolds' Store. Some men sat in tipped-back chairs on the wooden sidewalk. They were spitting tobacco juice and carving pieces of cedar wood into little piles of reddish-brown shavings. Sacks and boxes were piled on the sidewalk waiting to be loaded onto wagons. Two boys were playing, taking turns pushing each other off the sidewalk. Rose took Mama's hand.

As they passed from the bright sunlight to the darkness inside the store, Rose's eyes could see only shadowy shapes. But her nose instantly filled with a delicious riot of scents and smells. A tingle ran all through her body and settled in her stomach.

"Wait here, Rose," said Mama. Then she and Papa walked all the way to the back of the store to speak with Mr. Reynolds.

Slowly Rose's eyes began to see. She looked at what made all those smells. And she looked, and looked.

The store was a wonderland. Everywhere she turned were tables, shelves, rolls, bins, barrels, kegs, and boxes of every imaginable made thing in the world, all piled up every which way.

On the floor around her were sacks marked

Flour and Corn Meal, and bags of potatoes with the tops turned down. There were barrels brimming with pickles, and crackers, and raisins, and kegs of horseshoes and nails.

The dark wooden counters had moldings that seemed to frown down at her. On top there were piles of overalls, socks, pants, and men's hats. On other counters there were coffeepots, dishes, pitchers, and washbasins. There were boxes of seed packets painted with beautiful pictures of shiny red tomatoes, and dark green watermelons, and pale green cabbages.

The walls of the store were all made of shelves. Some drooped with great bolts of colored calicoes, gaily checked ginghams, dotted swiss, sleek silks, and shiny ribbons. There were boxes of different-colored sewing thread arranged like a rainbow, and piles of pencil tablets, schoolbooks, and slates.

There were rows of metal tins lined up like soldiers, and bottles of every size and shape, full of colored liquids, with brightly colored labels.

Even the ceiling had been used to hang water buckets, and tools, and horse collars.

Rose walked farther back into the store. Waves of scents washed over her and made her giddy. She took deep breaths of nutmeg, and coffee, and tobacco, and pickle brine, and onions, and coal oil, and paint, and leather.

A young man in a crisp white shirt was cutting a wedge from a big wheel of cheese. He pulled a sheet of paper from a long roll and tore it off to wrap the cheese. Then he pulled some string and cut it to tie the package up.

A woman was giving her order to another clerk, and he was writing it down on a piece of paper.

Rose stared as she passed jars and kegs crammed with brightly colored candy. She could smell the peppermint and it made her mouth water. There were perfumed candy bananas, and licorice sticks, and striped hard candy, and lemon drops.

"Hello there, young lady," a man's voice boomed out close by. "What can we do for you today?"

A man with a big belly stood with his hands on his hips, looking down at her. His big teeth grinned at her from under a bushy mustache.

"Which one do you like?" he asked.

Rose was startled. Her ears warmed. She didn't know what to say. The man laughed.

"It's all right," he said. "I'm Mr. Reynolds. This is my store. Your ma and pa are right over there, giving their order. How about these lemon drops. Do you like them?"

Rose nodded. She had never eaten a lemon drop, but she just knew she would like them.

The man pulled a little brown bag with red stripes on it from a rack. Then he took a tiny shovel and scooped up a whole scoopful of the sunny lemon drops. He poured them into the bag, folded the top, and handed it to Rose.

Her heart fluttered so, she almost forgot to say, "Thank you, Mr. Reynolds."

"You bet," Mr. Reynolds said. He called out to a customer and walked away.

Rose weighed the bag in her hand. It was heavy with lemon drops. She wanted to eat one right then, but she would wait to share with Mama and Papa on the ride home.

Mama was holding up a piece of cloth, brown calico with white polka dots.

"How do you like this, Rose?" Rose looked at the fabric. Then she looked at the other bolts of cloth on the shelves. Her eyes rested on a bolt of pale blue and pink gingham.

"I like that one," Rose said. The brown reminded her of mud. The gingham made her think of flowers.

"It's very pretty," said Mama. "But I don't think it will wear as well as the brown. It will show when it's soiled."

Rose had always worn calico. She thought she would like gingham, for a change. She looked at the blue and red, the blue and black, and at a dark blue and deep lavender.

"That one," she said, pointing to the blue and lavender. The clerk took down the bolt, measured out five yards, and cut it with a big shears. Watching him do it, Rose felt a wave of happiness. She had not had a new dress in almost a year, since Mama had sewn up the sprigged blue calico.

Rose wanted blue hair ribbons to go with her dress, but she knew not to ask. She could have new hair ribbons when Mama said so.

Finally they were finished and it was time to go home. Papa backed the wagon up to the sidewalk and loaded everything in. Rose's mouth watered when she saw the big bag of flour. They would have light bread again after a long winter eating corn bread day in and day out.

On the short ride home they ate some of the puckery-sweet lemon drops. The day had turned so warm that Rose had to take off her coat, now that no one would see the rip. The sky was clear and blue. A lone white cloud rose from the horizon in front of them.

In the wagon behind them were new shuck collars for the mules, spring onion sets, packages of seeds for the garden, seed potatoes, the coal oil can filled to the top with coal oil, a sack of sugar, a sack of flour, a box of salt, a tin of tea, a big piece of salt pork, a tin pail of molasses, the gingham for Rose's new dress, thread, a large piece of denim, and chambray for shirts. Mama said she would sew Papa a new shirt and pair of overalls. She would make a shirt and pair of overalls for Swiney, too.

"You see, Bess," Papa said. "Reynolds treated us square. We'll have everything we need to get through till settling up time in the fall, and then some."

Fighting Mules

As they came to the crest of the hill, the lone cloud seemed to grow taller, and to billow. It was a strange-looking cloud, Rose thought. It seemed to be coming from the ground, right on the wooded hill where the house and barn stood.

All at the same time, Papa whipped the reins and Mama cried out, "Manly, fire!" The horses jumped forward. The coal oil can shot backward through the wagon and crashed against the endgate. Bits of mud hit Rose's cheek.

The wagon flew down the bumpy tracks.

The horses' shod feet struck sparks on the stones. Rose's teeth clattered as she bounced on the hard seat. Mama stared at that cloud of smoke. Her face had gone white. Papa's mouth was set in a pale, thin line. Rose's stomach flip-flopped. No one spoke a word.

In no time at all the horses were grunting up the hill. Fido pranced down the wagon tracks to greet them, his tail wagging. As soon as the house came into view, Mama breathed a big sigh. Then they could see the barn as well. Everything looked as normal as could be.

"Praise be," Mama said in a trembly voice. "It's not on our place. It just looked that way. The smoke is coming from farther off."

"I'd best take a look," said Papa. "It's downwind from us, but you never can be too careful."

Papa unhitched May and rode into the woods toward the smoke, toward Mr. Kinnebrew's farm. Mama unhitched Pet and put her in the barn. Then Rose helped unload the wagon.

They watched that cloud of smoke every

minute. It grew smaller, and smaller, and paler. Finally only blue sky remained. Then Papa returned.

"It was only Abe, burning off one of Kinnebrew's brush piles," he said. "There was never any danger." But worry lines darkened his forehead.

"That's a relief," said Mama. "My heart was in my mouth when I saw that smoke."

"That's not all," said Papa. "He was also burning off the fields and even the woods, too. Just letting the fire burn through perfectly good timber."

"Whatever for?" Mama asked.

"It's the most confounded thing I ever heard. He says folks here always burn off the underbrush and new fields in spring. They just let the fires go till they burn themselves out."

"But why?" asked Mama.

"They say it improves the soil, and clears out the weeds and stump sprouts. But I don't like it," Papa said. "It's a crime to treat good land that way!"

The roughness in his voice startled Rose. It

was always so calm and patient. Even horses trusted Papa when he spoke. But fire was a monstrous thing. They were all terribly afraid of it. Rose still remembered the fire that had burned up their house in South Dakota many years before.

"We'll just have to be on our guard, is all," he said. "We can be thankful at least that the land here is good and wet. A fire can't travel far and do too much harm."

Now began the hard work of planting the garden. First Papa got out the harrow he had made during the winter. He sharpened the wooden teeth with his knife.

Then he hitched the harrow to the mules and they dragged it back and forth, breaking up the clods of earth into smaller and smaller clumps. Finally, after many passes, the garden was smooth and soft. Then he hitched the mules to the plow and plowed deep rows in the garden, leaving high ridges of dirt on either side.

Rose helped Mama cut the potatoes into small pieces, making sure each piece had at least two eyes. Then they carried them to the garden in a sack and buried the pieces in the ridges of dirt. They made sure the eyes were facing up. That way they could see the sun and sprout properly. They buried the bits of seed potatoes deep, where they would be safe and warm in case of a late frost.

Then they planted the onion sets and the turnip seeds. Mama planted the tomato seeds in soil she put in wooden hotbeds Papa had made. On warm days she brought the hotbeds out of the house and set them in a sunny place. She always made sure to bring them in before supper, so the cold nights couldn't hurt them.

Every day fires burned on farms all around them. The air was always full of wood smoke. No matter what she was doing, Mama would stop every so often and look around, through the trees at the columns of smoke. If she was inside, she would come outside to look. If she was crouched down in the garden, she would stand up, shield her eyes from the bright sunlight with her hand, and sniff the air. At night they could sometimes see the orange glow of a neighbor's burning brush pile or field.

"I just can't get used to the idea of it," Mama said to Papa at breakfast one morning. "I can't forget those terrible fires on the prairie, and how hard we fought to make the little cottonwood trees grow. People here treat trees like a nuisance."

"But you can't keep piling up the cut brush forever," said Papa. "There'd be no room for planting before long. We have to burn some of our brush piles, as well."

One day, after a soaking rain, Papa told Mama and Rose and Swiney to meet him in the orchard. He and Abe poured some coal oil on the great mounds of branches and stumps that had collected all winter. Then they lit them.

Papa told Rose and Swiney to watch that no sparks fell in the woods and started another fire. But the rain had wet everything down. No fire could start anywhere except where Papa wanted it.

So Rose and Swiney played around the great bonfires, watching them grow until long tongues of scorching orangey-red flame licked the sky. Terrified rabbits scurried out from where they had been living under the piles and bounded off into the woods with Fido chasing after them. Rose and Swiney tried to catch them, too. But the rabbits were too scared and too fast.

Papa did not try to shoot any of the rabbits. It was spring, when all the wild animals have their babies. There would be no more fresh meat until fall, when all the woods creatures had grown up.

Rose and Swiney threw sticks into the flames and watched them burn. They listened to the roaring and the popping and hissing. Then they pulled the sticks out and drew smoke pictures in the air. Their faces turned pink from the searing heat, and Rose burned her fingers playing with her stick. But she was having too much fun to care.

The fires burned all day. They took turns going back to the house to eat, so that someone always was watching. The fires burned into the night, too. Papa stayed to watch until the coals had cooled and no sparks came out. The next morning, all that was left was piles of ash and a few blackened tree limbs and smoking stumps, sticking up like the bones of a skeleton.

One beautiful, warm Sunday, after they got home from church and ate dinner, Mama said Rose must be good and watch the farm. She and Papa were going back into town, to see the Cooleys.

"Can't I go, too?" Rose pleaded. She never got a chance to play with Paul and George in church. They had to sit still and be quiet.

"No," said Mama. "Paul and George are staying behind also, to watch the hotel. We are going for a buggy drive, just Mr. and Mrs. Cooley, Papa and I."

Rose sat on one of the trunks by the bed and sulked while Mama quickly changed out of her good black cashmere into her white lawn. It was pretty and light, with a collar crocheted in pineapple shapes.

Rose pouted while Mama put extra wood in the little stove in the lean-to kitchen. Then she put in two loaves of bread to bake. They would be ready when she and Papa came home.

Papa saddled the mares, and Mama and Papa rode off toward town.

"Be good, Rose," Mama called out. "Don't wander off, and watch the stove."

Rose was bored. The first thing she did was take off her stockings and shoes. At least if she had to stay home alone, she could go barefoot. She put her shoes under the bed. Her feet were pale from being cooped up all winter. She wiggled her toes. They were happy to be free again.

"I'm not wearing shoes anymore till winter comes again," Rose told herself out loud.

Then she went outside and sat on a stump in the yard. She listened to the wind sighing in the trees. Far away a train whistled, grew close, and passed. The first tiny leaves were sprouting, tender and blushing pale pink and yellow and green. The air smelled fresh with the scent of newly turned earth.

Little white butterflies fluttered here and

there in the new grass. Bumblebees butted and buzzed, starting their nests. They landed on purple violets, bending the delicate flowers with their weight and nosing in them for nectar.

Goldfinches fluttered from tree to tree, calling out their spring cheer. A robin snatched up a tiny twig and flew away to the nest it was building high up in a tree.

Rose was bored again, so she decided to look at the mules. Papa had told her to stay away from them. But Rose thought she would just give them a little salt. The mules loved salt almost as much as they liked the tender young blades of new grass that were pushing up everywhere. Rose got a handful of salt from the house.

One of the mules was bay-colored, and the other was gray. Papa had named the bay mule Roy, for his big brother Royal. Mama named the gray mule Nellie, after a little girl she had known a long time ago.

When Rose walked into the hallway of the barn, the mules did not come to the stall gates to see her. They stood at the backs of their stalls, eyeing her suspiciously. Rose climbed up on the log wall and laid the salt on top of the low wall that separated their two stalls.

Both of the mules went straight to the salt. Nellie got there first, and when Roy tried to lick some, Nellie squealed horribly, wheeled around, and kicked at the log walls with all her might. Little chips of wood flew into the air. Roy backed up, his ears laid back, snapping at the air with big yellow teeth. Then Nellie wheeled around and started licking again.

The sound of their fighting and braying and squealing was horrible, but it struck Rose as funny, and she shrieked with laughter. She had never seen anything like it.

The mules fought and fought, each getting a little lick of salt now and again, until finally all the salt was gone. Rose had been terribly naughty. She blushed just to think of what Mama would say if she knew. But of course she wouldn't.

Rose was trying to think of something else to do when Swiney came riding up on Abe's mule, Old Guts. Rose could hear Old Guts' stomach rumbling as he walked. That was why they called him Old Guts.

"Howdy, Rose," Swiney called out, sliding off Old Guts' saddle. His foot got caught in the stirrup and he tumbled to the ground. Rose giggled. Swiney got up and brushed himself off. "What are you doing?"

"Nothing," said Rose. "Mama and Papa went riding. I was playing with the mules. They were fighting over salt. Do you want to see?"

"You bet," he said.

Rose got another handful of salt. This time the mules smelled the salt and started fighting before she even put it down for them. Swiney and Rose laughed and laughed. Then, when the salt was all gone, Swiney showed Rose how to imitate their squeals and braying. It made the mules fight again because they thought there was more salt.

While they were watching the mules fight, Swiney spat a stream of brown juice onto the ground.

"Abe lets you chew tobacco?" Rose asked in surprise. Chewing tobacco was a thing done by grown-up men. Mama did not approve of a man chewing tobacco. She said it was a disgusting habit, and once she had told Papa he'd better think twice before he ever took it up.

"Sure he lets me," said Swiney. "Abe lets me do anything. He ain't my pa."

"What does it taste like? Is it good?" Rose asked.

"It's all right, I reckon," Swiney said with a shrug. "It's just a thing to do."

Finally they tired of the mules. "Mules are mean," Rose said. "I like horses better. Does Old Guts fight?"

"Naw. He's tame as a kitty-cat. I been a-riding him since I was a baby. Want to ride him?"

"Could I?" Rose asked eagerly.

Swiney untied Old Guts and turned him so Rose could put her foot in the stirrup. Papa had let Rose sit on the mares a few times, and had led her around with the halter on Little Pet. But she had never ridden by herself.

Rose knew how to pull herself up. She

scrambled up on top of Old Guts and settled into the saddle. The mule turned and looked at her with baleful eyes.

"Go on," Swiney said. "Give him a kick."

Rose kicked her heels a little against the mule's sides.

"Aw, come on," Swiney said. "Kick him good."

Rose kicked harder, but Old Guts ignored her and nibbled some grass.

Swiney picked up a stick and swatted Old Guts on the backside with a *whap!*

The mule leaped into the air, tossing his head. Rose pitched forward and her forehead hit him hard between the ears with a clunk. Old Guts galloped a few steps, his stomach rumbling, and then stopped short. Rose's head spun. She climbed trembling down from the mule's back. She wobbled a few steps and then sat down hard.

Swiney came running. "What happened?" he shouted.

"I hit my head," Rose groaned. Everything was spinning.

"Uh-oh," Swiney said. "You're looking kind of puny, Rose. I'll fetch some water."

Rose sat there as still as she could for a long time. Swiney brought the wooden water bucket. Rose drank a dipperful. The cold, clean water refreshed her. The spinning slowed down, and then she just felt a little woozy.

"You look like a ghost, Rose," Swiney said.

Rose grinned weakly. She stood up on wobbly legs. Swiney picked up the water bucket and followed her to the house. Just as she got to the lean-to door, Rose smelled smoke. She remembered Mama's bread cooking in the stove. Out of the corner of her eye something made her look up.

She glanced at the chimney pipe coming out of the lean-to roof and gasped. Little flames were licking up from the lean-to roof, around the chimney opening. The roof was burning! The house was on fire! Rose's mind went black with horror.

Her breath snagged in her throat. Her legs turned to stone. She stood there in frozen terror, staring at the tiny orange flames that danced in the breeze. They were growing bigger even while she watched.

Then, suddenly, Rose snatched the bucket from Swiney's hand.

"Say," he shouted. "What's the idea?"

Rose raced around the back of the house. She ran to the edge of the gully where the spring was. She tripped on a root and tumbled down the path, splashing into the water. She got right up, scooped a bucketful, and scrambled up the slippery, muddy path. Her eyes stung. A sob jerked from her throat.

Swiney stood on the roof. He had taken off his shirt and was beating the fire with it.

"Quick, Rose!" he shouted. "Hand that bucket up. Hurry!" He squatted and leaned over the edge of the roof. It was low, but not low enough. The bucket was too heavy for Rose to lift all the way to Swiney's hand. Another sob strangled her breath.

She poured some water out. Then she lifted the bucket with all her strength in both hands. Swiney barely caught the bail in his fingertips.

He heaved the bucket onto the roof with a loud grunt. Then he poured the water all around the chimney. Steam and smoke mingled in the sunshine.

Rose peered inside the lean-to. Water ran sizzling down the outside of the stovepipe. It splashed and hissed on the top of the stove. It crackled inside the stove, where it put out the coals. The bread was ruined.

Rose sighed a great shivery sigh. There was no fire in the house. Only the roof had burned, and only a little.

She slumped against the doorway and sat on the sill. She put her face in her hands. She began to shake all over. Then she cried.

Swiney sat down next to her. They sat there a long time, Rose crying and Swiney saying nothing. Finally Rose snuffled up the last of her tears. She wiped her face with the hem of her skirt.

"I better go," said Swiney.

Rose walked with him to Old Guts, who was scrunching up some grass. Swine climbed up into the saddle and looked down at Rose.

"You shouldn't cry none," he said. "It's all right now."

"Thank you," said Rose. "You saved our house. If you hadn't gone up on the roof. . . . I don't know how you did it . . . I . . . I couldn't have reached it by myself." The thought of what might have happened brought tears welling in her eyes again.

"I just climbed up the logs," Swiney said, grinning. Rose had to smile a little herself.

Now Rose waited for Mama and Papa with a dreadful sinking feeling. They would be upset about the fire. And Rose had been very naughty, teasing the mules. A little bit of her even thought the fire might have been her own fault.

Rose was afraid she would cry when she tried to tell them. But she didn't.

"The roof caught fire from the stove," she said as soon as Mama and Papa rode close enough to hear. "But Swiney was here. He helped put it out."

Mama and Papa jumped down from the horses at the same time, their faces lined with worry.

"What! How in the world . . . " Mama blurted. She looked at the roof. Then she looked inside the lean-to, and inside the stove.

"Are you all right, Rose?" Papa asked.

Then Rose told Mama and Papa the whole story of that afternoon, except the part about feeding salt to the mules. She flushed hot with shame. She promised herself she would never do such a terrible thing again.

When she told about knocking heads with Old Guts, Papa guffawed loudly. Mama frowned at him. Rose didn't know what to think.

"Now, Bess," said Papa. "I'll bet you were some kind of shaken up, weren't you Rose?"

Rose nodded. Her forehead ached a little.

Mama bit her lip. Her eyes glimmered with tears, and she gave Rose a hug.

"It's my fault," Mama finally said. "Trying to save a little time by leaving that flimsy stove hot like that. The pipe sections must have come apart, letting the sparks get to the roof."

"Now, Bess, don't you fret so. It's just like your ma used to say, there's no loss without some gain. First thing, I'm going to tear down that old lean-to and build you a real kitchen, with a proper chimney."

The New Room

The next day Papa took the little stove out of the lean-to. Then he and Abe tore the lean-to away from the house, log by log. When they finished, there was nothing left but the hard bare ground that had been the lean-to floor, and the doorway into the house. Papa and Abe began to build a new, bigger room on that spot which would be the kitchen.

First they made a low stone wall, in the shape of a large box. One side of the box was the log house. The stone wall was the foundation. Rose and Swiney helped find stones that

Papa could fit snugly together to make it solid and level.

On top of the foundation they made another box by laying down four heavy squared-off logs of white oak. That was the sill. The sill must be good and sturdy to hold up the floor, the stove, and the walls. The stone foundation would keep the wooden sills from touching the ground, so they would stay dry and season hard.

Next they laid heavy joists across the sill, to hold up the floor.

But instead of building the walls out of logs, like the walls of the house, Abe helped Papa split logs into hewn clapboards. The clapboards were rough like shingles. They were thick on one edge and thinner on the other like shingles, too. They weren't as fine and smooth as sawed boards. But Papa said, "Abe is a mighty fine wood cobbler. Those walls will stand as long as time lasts."

"How long is that?" Rose asked.

"Nobody knows," said Papa.

While they worked, Abe sang and whistled

songs that Rose had never heard before. He called them frolic songs.

> *"Lips a-like a cherry,*
> *Cheeks a-like a rose,*
> *How I love that little gal,*
> *God A'mighty knows!*
>
> *"Get along home, Cindy, Cindy,*
> *Get along home, Cindy, Cindy,*
> *Get along home, Cindy, Cindy,*
> *I'll marry you sometime."*

"Why is it called a frolic song?" Rose wanted to know.

"On account of it's played at a frolic. Why else?" Swiney chimed.

"What's a frolic?"

"It's a time when folks get together and dance," Abe said, holding a board so Papa could nail it in place. "Of a Saturday night, some folks will clear the beds out of their house, wax the floor up real slick, and bid their neighbors and friends come by for a frolic. Some fellow, like me, comes up and fiddles, or picks the banjo. Then they all dance till their toes are a-twiddling in their boots."

Rose laughed and twiddled her toes.

"You never seen the like of it," said Swiney. "If it's a real good frolic, them big boys get to fighting over some girl."

A frolic sounded like fun. Rose wanted to see one, although she didn't think she wanted to see any fighting.

"Can we go, just one time?" Rose begged. "Just to see?"

"I think that a frolic is not something for little girls," Mama said politely.

In no time at all, the walls were up and the roof was on. Papa left two square holes, one in the east wall and one in the west wall. He made two wooden doors for those holes and hung them on leather hinges. When they were closed, the room was very dark.

"In the fall, when it gets cold again, we'll get you proper glass windows," Papa told Mama. "But for now, while it's warm, we can leave the shutters open during the day when you want the light."

"It's just beautiful the way it is," said Mama, her eyes bright with pleasure.

There was a hole in the roof, too, where the stovepipe would go. Papa said he would line the hole with tin, so the roof could never catch fire again.

Next Papa and Abe laid down the floorboards on top of the heavy joists. Rose noticed for the first time that the floor went right out the door and made a shelf outside, in front of the kitchen.

"The part outside is the porch," Papa said. "Now Mama can sit out outside like a lady and cool off on a hot summer day."

The last floorboard Papa laid down was short, and it was in the middle of the floor. The board had a hole in it, too, big enough to stick your fingers in. That board was a trapdoor. Mama could pull it up and store vegetables and eggs in the cool space under the kitchen.

Then, the last thing, Papa took the old door from the house and fitted it to the doorway of the new room. Finally Rose could walk all around the new room. She was sorry to see dirty footprints on the bright new floor. But it was beautiful and clean-smelling inside.

Rose noticed light peeking between the clapboard walls.

"Won't the wind come through when it's cold?" Rose asked Mama.

"We'll batten the walls with thin strips of wood," said Mama. "But the stove will warm it up when we're using it, and when we aren't, we'll be cozy in front of the fireplace in the house."

Mama and Rose swept all the dirt and sawdust out of the kitchen. Then they moved the table from the house into the kitchen, and laid one of the rag rugs over the trapdoor. Papa gathered up his tools and began to put them away.

"What about the stove?" Mama asked.

"It's getting late and I've got to feed and water the mares and mules," said Papa. "The weather's good. Why don't you cook outside? We'll move the stove tomorrow, after breakfast."

"Very well," said Mama. "But it isn't a very big job. It's just a small stove."

The next morning after breakfast, Papa said he had a load of fence rails to deliver in town. He was gone most of the morning. Mama and Rose hoed the garden to make new rows where they would plant beans and squash. Crows had been digging in the potato hills, eating the seed potatoes. So they had to cut and plant more.

"I wonder what can be keeping him?" Mama said as they worked. "I've got my dough ready to bake. But I don't want to start a fire in the stove if we're going to move it."

Finally, just as Mama had decided to go ahead and start dinner, they heard the wagon splashing across the ford on Wolf Creek and rumbling up the hill. Fido raced down the wagon tracks to meet it. The mares were grunting and slipping on the flinty stones, trying to pull the wagon. Papa had draped the oil-cloth covers over something in the wagon-box, which rode low on its springs.

"I wonder what that could be," said Mama,

mopping her forehead with the hem of her apron. She laid down her hoe and followed the wagon.

Papa drove right up to the kitchen porch and *whoa*ed the horses. He set the brake and jumped down. A grin crinkled his mouth.

"I can see you've got something up your sleeve," Mama said. "What is it?"

Papa climbed into the wagon-box and pulled off the oilcloth covers. Mama's mouth flew open. Sitting there, still half in its crate, was a brand-new cast-iron stove. Papa crossed his arms and waited for Mama to speak.

"Oh, Manly!" Mama cried out finally. Her hand flew to her mouth.

"It isn't the best stove money can buy," Papa said proudly. "But when I do a thing, I do it right. It's got a hot water reservoir. Now you can heat water and cook at the same time!"

The stove was beautiful. A pattern of sprigged flowers and leaves spread all over the doors. The nickel knobs and pins gleamed in the sunlight.

Rose waited for Mama's face to melt into

happiness. But her mouth was tight, and her forehead furrowed. Finally she said, simply, "No."

Papa's eyes widened. "No?" he said.

"Yes," said Mama, more firmly this time. "I mean no. I mean, you must take it back."

"What in tarnation?" Papa said.

"We cannot afford the expense," said Mama. "It's that simple. I couldn't bear to cook on it knowing we had gone into debt for it. You know how I feel. You will just have to take it back. I'm sorry. I know you only meant to please. But no."

Papa stared at Mama in disbelief. Rose held her breath. She had never heard Mama speak so to Papa.

"Now just a durn minute," Papa said, jumping down from the wagon. "I went to no end of trouble trading with Reynolds for fence rails and railroad ties. Prices are high now. There's never been a better time. One way or another, I'll pay for the blasted thing. Now quit this foolishness and let's get on with unloading it."

"Manly Wilder, you won't talk me into

98

anything by cussing," Mama said. Rose flinched. "You can unload it yourself. You can install it yourself. But I'll cook in the fireplace like my ma did before I'll cook on that stove. It's a sinful, wasteful extravagance for folks as poor as us.

"I have a perfectly good stove already," she said, pointing to the little tin stove sitting near the porch. "How can we ever get ahead if we keep going deeper and deeper in debt?"

Now Papa's face was deeply creased between the eyes. He stared at Mama for a long moment.

"Dash it all, Bess!" he shouted. "Hang the expense. What's the difference if we owe an extra twenty dollars? It may as well be two hundred. If we can't pay it, Reynolds will give us more time. But I gave my word and I don't aim to take it back."

Mama took a step back. "I just—" she began to say. But Papa's earnest voice drove on.

"See here," he said, "it's been more than fifteen years since I set out to find my fortune on the frontier. We can't live like sodbusters all our lives, letting the land grind us down year after year. I wouldn't wear out a dumb horse that way, not for any reason.

"Why should I let you wear yourself down, bending and slaving over a flimsy stove, worrying yourself half to death about fire? By jiminy, sometimes I . . . "

Then Papa ran out of words. He took his hat off and threw it to the ground, hard as he could. It landed with a puff of dust. Then he took a big breath, picked it up, and brushed it off.

"I've got work to do," he muttered. He turned and stalked off to the barn, forgetting to unhitch the team. Mama looked after him with a long face. Her hands wrung each other. Then she walked slowly into the kitchen.

Rose was dumbfounded. She had never seen Mama and Papa quarreling so. She had never heard Papa speak so forcefully. She didn't know what to think, or do, or say.

Even the horses seemed stunned, standing still as statues. Fido looked at Rose, his head cocked in a question. Then he trotted off to the barn after Papa. The yard filled with a terrible silence.

A gloom thickened around Rose and pressed down on her. She yearned to go off somewhere where she could be alone, and think. But she knew she shouldn't. Now was a time to be extra good, and quiet as a mouse.

She gathered kindling to cook dinner. She laid it next to the little camp stove where it sat outside near the porch. The sound of rattling pots came from the kitchen. Presently Papa came and unhitched the horses. After he led them away, Mama came out and lit a fire in the little stove.

Chickens

Dinner was dreadful. Mama and Papa did not speak to each another. Rose could not enjoy the beautiful new kitchen. The cozy clatter of dishes and utensils could not defeat the silence. Papa ate quickly and left to go work in the timber lot. Mama sighed after he had walked out the door.

"Well," Mama said after they had washed and dried the dishes. "It's time we cleaned out the henhouse. Two of the chickens have gone broody and I think one of them has stolen her nest out somewhere. Maybe you can find it for me."

Rose called Fido to help. She looked in the bushes near the house first. When Rose got down on her hands and knees to peek under them, Fido thought it was a game. He sniffed around the other side from where Rose was peering, a quizzical look on his face.

Then she hunted around the outside of the barn, and under a pile of brush that was left from when the barn had been built in the fall. But she found no nests.

It was wonderful to be outside. In the cabin the hearth fire had gone out for the last time. There were no more ashes to carry or wood to gather in the slushy mud and snow of winter. The door and windows stood wide to the spring. The log walls were no longer a shelter, but a prison opening to freedom with every dawn.

Spring was hazy on the Ozark hills. The skeletons of the trees were covering themselves in leaves. The brown slopes were burying themselves under drifts of green. White-oak leaves hung in rich masses. Black-jack leaves glittered in the morning sun. Little nuts were forming on the tufted walnuts.

The ground had finally begun to dry out. The dust of the path by the spring branch was velvety cool to Rose's bare feet. In the sunshine the flints were warm.

Papa had fenced in a small pasture, and the horses and mules had been turned out to graze. Baby quail were hatching. Squirrels and rabbits had their little ones.

Rose could not find the hen's nest.

"Either way, she'll show up one of these days with her babies," said Mama. "She's got awfully good sense. She has never lost a single chick for me. And Fido is such a good dog, he will watch out for her as well."

Next they cleaned out the henhouse. They swept out all the dirty litter from the floor. They emptied all the old straw out of the nest boxes that hung on the henhouse wall. Mama took out the roosting perches. She dabbed coal oil on the perches and in the cracks in the walls of the henhouse to kill lice and mites.

Then they put down a blanket of fresh leaves, mixed with wood chips and sawdust.

Mama put fresh straw in all the nest boxes. She showed Rose how to make sure each nest had a cozy little hollow in the middle.

"It should be deep enough so the eggs won't roll off to the side and get cold," Mama explained. "But not so deep that a clumsy hen will step on the eggs and break them."

Then she brought two white china doorknobs from the house that she had kept in one of the trunks. She set one in each of two nests. The hens would think they were eggs and lay their eggs in with them, instead of hiding them in the woods.

"That old rooster is starting to wear out," Mama said, looking over the flock as she fed them their ration of corn. "I'll have to find a young one. Maybe I can trade some chicks with Mrs. Stubbins. She has such nice Leghorns."

Rose thought chickens were not very smart and, except for roosters with their shimmering colored feathers, not pretty to look at. She couldn't play with them, or teach them tricks.

"Mama, why do you like chickens so well?"

Rose asked. "They take so much care."

"A chicken is a miracle of nature," said Mama. "And the salvation of any farm. A hen asks very little: a dry, safe place to sleep at night, sunlight, fresh air, water, some mash every day, and a place to scratch for worms and bugs and grasshoppers.

"In return, she is a factory for food. She gives us eggs for nearly two years. She gives us young pullets to fry up for Sunday dinner. And when she is old and tired, she cooks into a delicious stew with dumplings.

"Just think of it; a good chicken will lay an egg every day. Now I have twenty hens. If they lay a dozen eggs each day, and Mr. Reynolds will give nine cents the dozen, how much is that after a week?"

Rose was better at reading and writing than at arithmetic. She had to think a minute before she answered, "Sixty-two cents?"

"Sixty-three cents," Mama corrected. "Now, how much do you think that is after a month?"

That was too complicated a problem. "Two

dollars and more than four bits," Mama said. Rose looked at her in surprise.

"And in a year," Mama said, as she showed Rose how to multiply again, "that makes about thirty dollars."

Rose thought for a moment. Then she cried out, "Mama, that's more than the cost of the stove!"

The shadow of a frown flickered in Mama's blue eyes. Then she brushed away the numbers she had drawn in the dust.

"Yes, it is," she said. "But chickens are not predictable. They get sick, and remember last winter when that owl carried off my best layer? There are hawks waiting to carry off the spring pullets, and snakes to steal the eggs. And besides, we have many other things to pay for.

"Well, never mind about that now. Let's get back to work on the garden. We need to get those fence rails up if we're to keep the chickens from eating it up."

While they were working, Papa came back to the house with Abe. They climbed up into the wagon where it still stood by the porch.

Rose tried not to stare, but she couldn't help it. Papa and Abe slid the cast-iron stove out of the wagon. Then they dragged it across the porch, into the kitchen.

After that, there was nothing to see. But Rose heard the sound of metal banging, and hammering. After a time, the round chimney pipe poked up through the roof hole Papa had made and lined with tin. Rose stole sidelong glances at Mama, but Mama never looked up at the house. She just kept working, lifting fence rails and fitting them together.

When it was time for supper, Mama built a fire in the tin stove outside. Supper was almost as quiet as dinner had been. Only now, sitting in a corner of the kitchen was the shiny new stove. Rose dared not open the heavy iron doors, or lift any of the four covers on top.

When she had finished helping Mama with the dishes, Rose went to the barn in the gathering twilight to watch Papa doing his evening chores. He pitched fresh straw into the stables.

"How's my little prairie Rose tonight?" said Papa. "How do you like that new stove?"

Rose's face grew warm. She stammered from not knowing what to say.

"That's all right," said Papa, setting down the pitchfork. "I must have given you quite a fright, carrying on so. Were you scared?"

"A little," Rose said. "You never did that before."

"No, I never did," said Papa, his eyes wrinkling into a smile. "Hopefully never will again. Your mama's strong-willed, is all. Always was. Fact is, it's what I liked about her from the first. She's got spunk and spirit."

Then Papa looked at Rose with mirth in his eyes. "If you can keep it a secret, I'll tell you a nickname your grandpa used to call Mama."

"What!" Rose shouted with a giggle.

"Shhhh!" Papa shushed. "You must keep it a secret."

"I will," Rose whispered loudly.

"Just between us?" he said.

"Yes!" Rose nearly squealed.

"Flutterbudget," Papa said.

"What?"

"Flutterbudget," said Papa again. "When

your mama was young and she'd get her dander up, your grandpa teased her by calling her Flutterbudget."

Rose giggled. She couldn't imagine anybody calling Mama such a funny name. But she thought it sounded a little like Mama. Rose liked it.

"All right, now," said Papa with a wink. "That's the last word on the subject."

"But can we keep the stove?" Rose asked.

"That's for Mama to decide," said Papa. "We must wait and see."

Rose walked back to the house. Just as she was about to walk into the kitchen, she heard the metal clank of a stove door closing. When she walked in, Mama was patting down her apron and looking around as if she had lost something.

"Here, Rose," she said, snatching the broom from its place in the corner. "Sweep out the kitchen. Then it's time for your lessons."

Rose's heart grew lighter with each swish of the broom. Having a secret with Papa made her feel grown-up. She understood that everything would turn out all right.

Going Fishing

Rose woke in the fresh dawn to a chorus of birdsong and clattering stove lids. She smelled wood smoke, coal oil, and coffee. She heard the crackling sound of a fire. Her eyes popped open.

Rose leaped out of bed and threw off her nightgown. She wriggled into her dress and peered around the corner of the door. On the table, sprouting from a glass jar, was a beautiful bouquet of flowers.

Mama was bent over in front of the new stove, poking a stick of wood into the firebox. Sour-milk biscuits sizzled in a hot greased pan. Rose's heart jumped for joy.

"Good morning, Rose," Mama said cheerfully. "Look at the flowers Papa picked this morning."

The bouquet was lovely. There was a thin, twisted tree branch of white cross-shaped flowers. The outer edge of each petal was tinged reddish-brown, and the middle had a cluster of tiny seeds. "What's that?" Rose asked.

Mama said it was a kind of tree. "I've never seen it before," she said. "Papa said it grows down in the woods, on the other side of the timber lot."

There were tiny purple violets in the bouquet, and pink-edged spring beauties, and delicate yellow buttercups, and blushing purple blossoms of some sort, and sweet williams. The flowers and birdsong and the cozy warmth of the new stove in the corner made a merry breakfast. Mama and Papa did not speak of the stove, but when Papa came in to eat, he looked at Rose and winked.

After breakfast, Mama put a dried-apple pie to bake in the oven. They would take it with them to church the next day. Mama was also going to bake a chicken pie, the next morning.

Sunday was Decoration Day and there would be a church picnic. Rose jumped for joy. A picnic, with Paul and George!

"It isn't just for having fun," Mama said. "Decoration Day is when the church members weed and tidy up the graveyard. But it will be fun, too," she added.

Papa helped Mama and Rose finish the fence around the garden. They wove sticks through the lower rails to keep out rabbits and groundhogs. The sun was bright, and soon the day grew warm and smothery like summer.

Papa made a little log gate for the garden fence that fastened with a loop of rope on the top. When they were done, the garden looked very safe. No wild hogs could get in to root up the tender young plants.

Then Mama stretched pieces of string between the fence tops, across the garden. She tied scraps of cloth to the strings. The fluttering scraps would scare away crows and other birds.

At noon, when it was time for dinner, they

were all hot and thirsty. When they sat down to eat, Papa had a surprise.

"How would you girls like to go fishing this afternoon?"

"Fishing?" Rose had never been.

"Abe says he knows a good spot up on Wolf Creek," said Papa. "I could do with some fresh fish for a change."

So Papa hitched the mares to the wagon and they drove past the Kinnebrews' farm. Abe and Swiney were waiting for them at the end of the lane, by the wagon track. Abe was carrying his fiddle. As soon as they had climbed into the wagon box, he plucked the strings, tuning it up. Swiney got out his knife and sharpened it. Fido sat on Mama's lap where he could see everything better.

"I thought you folks might fancy a bit of music to pass the while," said Abe.

"That would be wonderful," Mama said. Abe drew the bow and began to play a lively song with simple words they could learn right away.

"Lark in the morning, sailing from her nest,
Lark in the morning, sailing from her nest,
Lark in the morning, sailing from her nest,
Dew-drops falling from her snow-white
    breast.

"The higher she flies the sweeter she'll sing,
The higher she flies the sweeter she'll sing,
The higher she flies the sweeter she'll sing,
And we'll all turn back to the green fields
    again."

Their voices rang out through the bare trees. The strong light made a lacy pattern through the tiny spring leaves. If Rose squinted her eyes, the woods looked like fall. But the gentle warm breeze and drowsy scent of the growing earth spoke only of the coming summer.

On the limbs of the still-bare oaks the wise squirrels ran fearlessly, frisking tails and cocking saucy eyes. Fido's ears perked up, and the squirrels scolded, "Chit! Chit! Chit!"

Then the wagon passed trees blooming a

purple haze. Those were the same flowers in Mama's bouquet. Abe said it was redbud. The little blossoms were bunched up all along the branches. Up close they looked like swarms of little purple bees with delicate pink wings.

Here and there in low places stood a few short trees with twisting branches, lighting the forest with snowy drifts of blossom. Those were the white flowers in Mama's bouquet.

"That there's dogwood," said Abe.

Finally the road ran by a large, deep stream and the wagon stopped. That was Wolf Creek. Great tall trees lined the banks. Their tangled roots, like gnarled toes, stuck out of the mud at the water's edge. A flock of brown birds that had been pecking in the mud flew up into the trees. Their bottoms flashed white. Their open wings showed golden yellow.

In a swampy place next to the creek, Abe showed them where a grove of cane grew. Swiney used his sharp knife to cut everyone one of those slender trees. The cane stems had little knuckles on them, and they were hollow inside.

They stripped all the delicate branches and feathery leaves from the cane. Papa and Abe tied long pieces of heavy sewing thread on the ends. Close to the ends of the threads they tied little bits of wood. Then they tied hooks on the ends of the threads.

Swiney showed Rose how to find bait. That was a game. They peeked under old rotting logs and found pale grubs, and slithery worms, and small slippery salamanders. Fido played, too. He pawed through the rotted soil, sniffing and sneezing.

Swiney took a worm and poked his hook through it. The worm squirmed and fought to get away, but it was stuck there.

"Here," Swiney said, giving Rose a worm. "Stick your hook in real good."

The worm waved and writhed in Rose's fingers, making itself short and fat, then long and thin. She hated the feel of it. She hated to hurt the worm by sticking the hook through it. She tried, but the worm kept slithering away. It stretched and stretched until it was impossibly skinny. She jabbed at it, but the hook

stuck her finger instead.

"Let me help you with that," said Papa. He took the worm in his hand, and with a flick of his fingers the worm was wriggling on the hook.

Now they spread out along the bank to fish. Mama sat on an old log, pushed her bonnet back, and watched. "It's so peaceful here," she said. "I'm perfectly content to sit and enjoy it."

Rose stood on the bank, at the edge of the water, and dropped her line in.

"Not like that," said Swiney. "The fish can see you. You got to be sneaky or they ain't going to bite. Come on."

They walked a little way upstream along the broad deep creek, hiding like Indians behind the bushes and logs along the banks. Then Swiney told Rose to hunch down. When they were almost flat on the ground, Swiney said, "Just crawl up close, but keep your head down. Then whip your pole over and let the hook fall in."

Rose flicked her pole back, and then forward. She felt something pulling right away. She peeked to see if the hook had fallen in the creek. But the thread was pointing behind her. Then she felt it, tugging in her dress. Swiney unstuck her and showed her how to cast her bait.

Finally, they were really fishing.

"How do you know if you caught one?" Rose asked.

Swiney laughed. "You'll know," he said. "The little hunk of wood starts to bob. Then the fish yanks your line like he's a-going to drag you right in the water." Rose grabbed the pole tightly with both hands.

They lay there in the leaves. Rose was impatient. She peered over the edge of the bank. Her line disappeared into the water. The piece of wood floated calmly. She lifted up, to see if there were any fish on the hook. But there was only the worm, still wriggling. She sighed and dropped it back in. Then she picked it up again. Still no fish. Downstream she could hear the low voices of Papa and Mama and Abe. She checked again. Nothing but the worm. Now it was limp.

Rose noticed a blood blister on her wrist that had not been there a moment ago. The blood blister wriggled a little. It had legs! Rose had to scrape and scrape at it to scrape off that flat brown bug. Swiney said it was a tick.

Rose scratched a bite on her leg. She watched spots of sunlight dancing on the water. Dead leaves floated lazily by. A breeze stirred, roughing up the water's surface.

Rose lifted her pole again. This time something pulled back. She jerked the pole hard. Something was holding it down.

"I got one! I got one!" Rose shouted. She could hardly breathe, she was so excited. She stood up and yanked as hard as she could. Then Swiney helped. He took the pole and pulled.

"Wait a minute," he said. He waded into the creek and fished around in the water with his hand. Then he pulled up Rose's hook. At the end was a stick, covered with dead leaves. The worm was gone.

"Let's go upstream, where that old dead

tree is hanging out over the water," said Swiney. "Them fish cain't look up and there won't be no sticks out there."

Now they sat out high over the water and dropped their lines into Wolf Creek. Rose liked fishing better when she could see the whole creek. She could see Abe and Papa fishing way downstream. In a shallow place, Fido was catching a fish that was trapped on a gravel bar. He grabbed it in his mouth and trotted off into the woods to eat it.

Abe had caught a fish and was taking it off the hook. Then he held it up by its tail. The dripping silver fish flashed like a knife blade in firelight.

Rose could see the dark shadows of fish swimming in the creek. She could even see fish come to look at her hook. But none of them wanted it.

She looked out on the creek. A fallen log on the far bank was covered with bumps. The bumps were turtles, lined up in a row, sunning themselves and catching flies.

Suddenly, right behind them on the bank,

Rose heard a loud splash. A long, slinky brown creature climbed up on the mud. It had beautiful shiny-wet fur on its arched back, and a pointed face, and whiskers. It shook itself like a dog. Then it looked around and scampered off into the woods.

"What was that?" Rose asked.

"Mink," said Swiney. "He's scared the fish away. Maybe we can catch something by noodling."

"Noodling?" Rose asked.

"I'll show you," said Swiney.

He climbed down from the dead tree and walked along the creek bank to a log that had fallen into the water. Rose watched from her perch.

"Sometimes the fish hide in here," he said. Swiney rolled his pants up and waded into the water along the log. When he got to the hollow end, he climbed up and sat on the log. Then he leaned over and stuck his hand under the water, into the hollow part.

He reached around inside for a moment.

"Cain't feel nothing," he said. "Wait! I

think there's something in there!"

He leaned over, to get his hand farther in. "Something's in there!" he shouted. His head was almost in the water, he had to reach so far in.

Then he shouted, "Got it!" He pulled his hand out of the water. Something was writhing in the splashing water. It was long and . . .

"Look out!" Rose shouted. "It's a snake!" Swiney had it by the tail.

"Jiminy!" Swiney screeched. He flung the snake away from him. It landed in the water with a plop. Then it swam wriggling away across the creek, its head poking out of the water.

Swiney stumbled and splashed out of the creek. He clambered up onto the bank, his eyes big and round. He was shaking. He looked at his hands and his arms. But the snake had not bitten him.

"Jiminy!" he said again. "I ain't never noodled no snake before. Jiminy!"

Rose was watching Swiney so intently, she didn't notice the tugging on her fishing pole. Then, all of a sudden, it nearly jumped out of her hands. She grabbed tight.

Her line slashed the water, this way and that. She could see the shadow of the fish. Its bright belly sparkled as it turned and fought the hook.

"I got one!" she shrieked.

She yanked on her pole, but that fish fought hard. The pole bent way over until she thought it might break. The fish dashed out into the middle of the creek. Rose gripped the tree trunk with her legs to keep from falling off.

"Don't jerk so hard!" Swiney shouted. "The hook will come out."

The fish fought and fought, but soon it tired and floated near the surface. Then Rose swung her pole over by the bank, where Swiney grabbed the line and unhooked it. It was a big fish with beautiful gold and blue scales and wide surprised-looking eyes. Swiney strung it through the gill on a piece of vine.

Rose ran downstream, carrying the still flopping fish by the piece of vine. "Papa, Mama, look!" she shouted.

"You got yourself a pretty little smallmouth there," said Abe.

Rose showed the fish to Mama and Papa.

"That will make good eating tonight," Papa said. Rose beamed. He took the fish and strung it with the fish he had caught. Rose counted. She and Papa had caught seven fish! And Abe had caught five fish for himself and Swiney. Swiney hadn't caught any.

Rose was proud as a gander. It made her feel good to help put food on their table.

They all fished a little while longer, but the fish had stopped biting. Finally Papa said it was time they got back to do chores.

He put all the fish in the keg he had brought, with water to keep them fresh. Then they all climbed back in the wagon and drove home. Great piles of white clouds mounted in the hazy blue sky. The air seemed to press down, hot and sticky.

"Looks like we might get some rain," said Mama. "We could use it, too. The garden is drying out."

"Most likely it'll be a gully-washer, too," said Abe. "I seen a couple snakes heading for high ground this morning. And the rocks in my corn patch was a-sweating dew. Them is sure signs a good rain is a-coming."

"We had better hurry and get the chores done soon as we get home," said Mama.

Rose pulled the string of fish out of the barrel of water, to see her fish again. She knew exactly which was the one she had caught.

"Sakes alive. That's the fourth time you've looked, Rose," Mama said. "You're going to wear those poor fish out before I get a chance to clean them."

Abe tuned his fiddle again and began to play and sing. The song was a story.

> *"Down in the Missouri mountains*
> *Far from the cares of the world,*
> *Stood Dan Kelly's son and he leaned on his*
>   *gun,*
> *Thinking of Zeb Turney's gal*

> *"Dan was a hotblooded youngster,*
> *His paw raised him sturdy and right.*
> *A gun he had worn since the day he was*
>   *born,*
> *To shoot every Turney on sight."*

The sky darkened and the wind picked up as they dropped Abe and Swiney off at the Kinnebrews'. Papa hurried the horses, to beat the coming storm home.

The Flood

Papa unhitched the team and put the horses in the barn. Then he brought the mules in from the little pasture.

The sky closed in, shutting out the last rays of sunlight. The forest grew dim and murky with an early dusk. The undersides of the dark clouds boiled. Thunder grumbled in the distance. Rose's heart beat with a strange excitement, and she felt feverishly hot. The sound of beating wings startled her. She looked up to see a flock of crows fleeing before the storm.

"It smells like hail," Mama said. "Let's get

the chickens inside."

She rattled a spoon in a bowl the way she always did at feeding time. The chickens came running with their necks stretched out, flapping their wings. Soon the yard was alive with scratching, quarreling, cackling chickens.

Rose helped Mama herd them into the henhouse. Just as the last chicken went in, Fido burst out barking from behind the large rock at the head of the spring. A moment later, Mama's missing hen strutted into the yard, all ruffled and cackling loudly. Behind her, running to keep up, was a little parade of fluffy chicks, eleven in all. Behind them was Fido, herding them toward the henhouse!

"What a good dog!" Mama exclaimed. "The rain might have washed the poor things away. But the baby chicks are too little to sleep in the henhouse."

She caught the hen and put her in the wire coop. The hen growled and pecked Mama's hand. But when the little peeping chicks crowded in around her, she sat down and preened herself.

The Flood

Mama laid down old newspapers in a corner of the kitchen. Then she set the coop on top of the newspapers. She put in a bowl of water and another bowl with cornmeal. The chicks crowded into the bowl, trampling the cornmeal and peeping excitedly.

"We will keep them in the kitchen until the weather clears up," Mama said.

The black clouds tumbled and rolled. The wind began to bend the tree branches and thrash the young leaves. The first drops of rain spattered dark spots in the dust as Rose raced to bring in extra stove wood.

Papa tipped the rain barrel over to dump out the old, stale water. Then he put it where it could catch rain running off the roof. Mama did not like to wash with spring water. Rain made better suds and it took less soap.

When all the animals were safe and snug and there was plenty of stove wood piled up on the porch, they all went inside and shut the door. Fido turned around three times and curled up next to the stove.

Rose peeked out the glass window in the

house. A tongue of lightning licked at Patterson's Hill just across the valley. The thunder boomed loudly. It seemed caught among the hills, unable to escape, rolling and echoing. Then the rain came rushing into the valley. It drummed loudly on the roof and poured off like water from a boot.

It beat so hard that Rose barely heard Mama call her to help with supper. Then hail fell, rattling as though someone were throwing rocks on the roof. The wind howled through the trees. It clawed at the walls and rattled the shutters in the kitchen. It shrieked down the chimney. It banged the damper in the stove.

The wild sounds of the storm made Rose shiver. She wanted to climb into bed and pull the covers over her head.

"It's just a rainstorm, Rose," Mama nearly had to shout. "Come and help me clean these fish."

Mama cut off all the heads. There were two perch, four fat catfish with long whiskers, and Rose's smallmouth bass. Mama showed Rose how to clean out the insides. Then she let

Rose scrape the scales off the bass she had caught. The scales sparkled like jewels in the lamplight.

Mama sprinkled cornmeal on the cleaned pieces and fried them in drippings in the skillet. When they had turned golden brown, she put them on the serving plate and sprinkled a few drops of vinegar over them. Then she fried the wild greens she had picked that day at Wolf Creek. The last thing she did was make a flour gravy to sop up with corn bread.

Finally they ate the delicious, delicate fish. It melted in Rose's mouth. She was hungry, and she ate and ate to fill the emptiness inside her.

The hail stopped and only rain pounded on the roof all through supper. The dampness made the house stuffy. But the wind was blowing too hard to open the door or the shutters. They could hear broken branches and twigs rattling and sliding down the roof.

It was Saturday, so after dinner they took their baths. Rose always bathed first. Mama set the tub near the stove and filled it partway with warm water. The splash of the water pouring into the tub and the splash of the rain pouring on the earth were one sound in Rose's ears.

Papa went into the bedroom to read a letter he had gotten from his sister, Rose's Aunt Eliza.

When Rose was done and Mama had checked her neck and ears, Mama freshened the bath with warm water from the reservoir. When she had finished bathing, she freshened it again for Papa. Papa always took his bath last, because he was the dirtiest.

While Papa bathed in the kitchen, Rose looked out the window of the bedroom again. She rubbed a little clear spot in the fog that had collected on the glass. It was pitch black outside, except now and then when a flash of lightning showed the trees bending and flailing in the wind. After that all she could see was running drops of rain, and light reflected from the lamp on the mantel.

Rose noticed a new sound, a roaring.

"What is that?" Rose asked.

Mama listened "It must be the spring, flooding from all the rain."

When Papa was done bathing, Rose played with the baby chicks. She cupped one of the tiny trembling creatures in her hand. It peeped loudly for its mother. Then the warmth of her hand made it drowsy. It blinked sleepily and looked up at her, its little head bobbing. Rose could feel its fragile, bony body and its rapid breath through the downy ball of its feathers.

Then she kissed its head and set it on the floor. The chick peeped and tottered about comically. It walked right in front of Fido's head, which was resting on his paws. The chick looked at Fido and peeped at him. Fido's ears perked up and he sniffed at it. Just then the chick pecked Fido's nose. Fido jerked back in surprise. He looked at Rose with a startled face that made Rose laugh.

"That bullheaded sister of mine is trying to talk my whole family into moving to Louisiana," Papa said. "She's so determined, she just might do it, too."

"I suppose Eliza Jane is a bit lonely, down there by herself with a new husband," said Mama. "And now with a baby due."

"She's already talked my little brother, Perley, into it. He's on his way there now by boat down the Mississippi, from Minnesota," said Papa. "He's going to be a rice farmer. Now she wants the rest of us to move down there as well."

"We're staying where we are," Mama said firmly. "I have moved enough times, and left behind enough gardens for the rabbits, for three lives. Wherever would she get the idea we would even consider it?"

"You know Eliza," said Papa. "She was your teacher once. Nobody has to give Eliza Jane any ideas. She's got plenty all on her own. I wouldn't be surprised if my mother and father took her up on it, too."

Just before bedtime, Papa lit the lantern and went to check the barn. It was still raining hard. When he came back he had a worried look on his face.

"This is a bad storm," he said. "The whole

136

ground is running like a river. There are a lot of tree limbs blown down. Fry Creek is over its banks."

They went to bed with an uneasy feeling. The rain lashed the window. The roaring of the spring and the creek was loud now. Rose was tired, but the drumming on the roof kept her awake.

She had just drifted off when the squeak of the lantern globe woke her up. Papa struck a match to light it. Mama was looking out the window. Her forehead was knobby with worry.

"Is it morning?" Rose asked.

"No," said Papa. "I heard a noise. I'm going to take a look."

Papa had been gone only a few moments when he came back in. His shoes were muddy and water poured off his hat. He shook himself like a sparrow.

"It's the henhouse," he said in a grim voice. "A tree fell on it."

"Oh, no!" cried Mama. "Is it bad?"

"I'm afraid so," said Papa. "We'll have to move them into the barn. Otherwise they may drown in this downpour, or catch a chill at the least."

"Get dressed, Rose," Mama said quickly.

Rose hurriedly pulled on her dress. Then she and Mama followed Papa out the door, into the driving rain and the inky blackness. Big drops of rain stung her face, like bullets fired by the wind. In an instant she was soaked to the skin. The wind howled in the trees. The rushing water of the spring roared in her ears.

She could feel mud squishing between her bare toes. The air smelled like newly plowed earth and freshly cut wood.

It was just a few steps to the henhouse. When the circle of lantern light fell on it, Rose gasped. A great tree had toppled over, right onto the roof. The sturdy little henhouse was crushed in half. The tree trunk blocked the door. She could hear the chickens squawking inside.

Papa fetched the ax and two-handled saw from the barn. Rose held the lantern while he and Mama sawed the tree in half. When they had cut almost all the way through the trunk, there was a loud cracking sound. The trunk twisted and began to roll off the henhouse toward Mama. The chickens squawked in fright. The henhouse leaned as if it were going to fall on her.

Rose tried to shout, "Look out!" But the water ran off her hair, down her nose, and into her open mouth. Nothing came out.

"Watch it, Bess!" Papa shouted.

At the last moment, Mama jumped out of the way. The tree trunk splashed in the mud right at her feet. The henhouse walls sagged. Now it was not a henhouse anymore. It was an old pile of wet logs.

Papa and Mama began to pull loose logs away, one at a time. When they had made a hole in the pile of logs, Papa took the lantern and looked in. Over his shoulder Rose could see some chickens huddled in a pile.

Papa began to hand chickens out to Mama, one at a time. Mama gave the first two to Rose.

"Take these and wait for me," she said. The chickens were soaked and muddy and they smelled rank. They were too terrified to struggle or flap their wings. Rose took one in each arm. Then Mama took three in her arms, and Papa picked up three more.

Then he held up the lantern and they walked through the squishy mud and pools of water to the barn. The wavering light lit the faces of the horses and mules and shone in their dark eyes as they poked their curious heads over the stall gates to see.

Papa set the wet hens in the damp straw on the hallway floor.

"We had best put them in the loft where they'll be safe and dry," he said. He climbed partway up the ladder. Then Mama handed him the chickens and he set each one in the soft, dry hay.

Then they went back for more. They made three trips altogether. They saved seventeen of Mama's hens. The old rooster was dead, and so were six of the young chickens.

"Thank goodness we kept the baby chicks inside," said Mama. "They never would have gotten through it."

When they were finished they walked by the spring to look. The lantern light was too weak to reach across the gully, but they could see foamy water boiling halfway up the sides.

"Be careful!" Mama shouted. "It's slippery here." She pushed Rose away from the edge with her hand. Rose was astonished to see how high up the thrashing water reached. The rain had turned the purling little spring into an angry torrent.

Then they walked down the wagon tracks toward Fry Creek. Rose could not see into the blackness. But when they had walked only halfway, she heard an even deeper, more terrifying roar. She noticed a wet, slapping, gurgling sound. Then, suddenly, her feet were in water!

"Mama! Papa! Look!" Rose cried out.

Fry Creek, which Rose could usually walk across in her bare feet, had climbed all that way up the wagon tracks toward the house. They stared into the darkness. All they could see in the lantern light was the black, rippling water. It lapped against the nearest tree trunks and foamed around the bushes. Rose could not picture it, but she knew the valley must be one great river! They would never get to Decoration Day now.

Somewhere out in that horrible flood they heard the piteous bawling of a cow. Rose shivered.

"Do you think we're in any danger?" Mama shouted. "It's awfully high. Maybe we should move the livestock up the ridge."

"No," Papa said. "We're safe up here. But I better check on the neighbors when it's light. I reckon some of them will need help."

Baby Birds

Mama made an early breakfast in the dark. As soon as the first smudge of light showed in the window, Papa saddled one of the mules and rode off toward Kinnebrew's.

"If anybody needs a hand today, it'll be the folks downstream," he said. Mr. Stubbins' farm was upstream, on higher ground.

Mama and Rose hurriedly washed the dishes. Then they went outside to look at the flooded land. Shattered tree limbs lay everywhere on the ground. It was still raining, though more gently now than during the night. The rain barrel overflowed. Fog and mist hung in the treetops. The voice of the wind was stilled.

The henhouse was ruined, a pile of rubble. Mama fed and watered the chickens in the hallway of the barn.

"This is a bother," said Mama. "They were so stirred up last night they probably won't lay for a week."

The garden was all piles of mud and pools of water. Little rivers had cut swirling paths through the middle, washing away some of the seeds and tender shoots. Here and there seed potatoes, their tender shoots sticking up, peeked out of the wet ground. A large limb had fallen on the fence and broken it down.

"We have our work cut out for us," Mama said with a weary sigh. "I reckon we'll have to replant. The potatoes will rot in this dampness. At least we have the tomato plants still in the hotbeds. We can plant them as soon as the soil dries out."

All over the ground, little brown toads were hopping. There were so many the earth seemed alive and moving. Fido chased one, trying to catch it in his mouth. Rose caught one in her hand. Its tiny eyes looked without blinking. Its frowning mouth bulged underneath and puffed with every breath. Its brown skin was covered with warty bumps.

Rose looked up to see Fido sitting in front of her. He cocked his head quizzically and raised an ear. Rose looked at him. His face had an expression Rose had never seen.

"What is it?" she asked him.

Fido's other ear perked up. Then he opened his mouth. Out jumped a toad!

Then she and Mama walked down the wagon track to the flood's edge. Water rippled around the tree trunks. Beyond the trees they could see the brown plain of the flood. The swirling water was the color of dirty cream, spreading out as if poured from a pitcher. It boiled in places like stew.

Mama shook her head slowly. "Land sakes," she finally said. "The railroad must be washed out as well. I never heard the whistle of Number Six this morning. I wonder how the Cooleys are doing. Decoration Day must certainly be rained out."

"At least there isn't a drought anymore," Rose said, remembering the years of dry weather where they used to live, in South Dakota.

Mama chuckled. "Just think. Last summer we were choking on dust. Then the fires, and now this. As Papa says, if it isn't chickens, it's feathers."

Waves of churning, roiling water raced by. Fry Creek, only yesterday sparkling peacefully among the rocks, had vanished. Rose could not tell where it flowed.

In its place, the flood covered everything. You couldn't see an inch into the murky water. No one could ever cross it alive. Rose stared at the flowing water so long it made her dizzy. When she looked away the earth seemed to slide backward.

Everything the flood had stolen from the land hurtled past them on the waves: brush, boards, chicken coops, a drowned muskrat, fence rails, railroad ties, split wood, bottles.

Rose wondered about all the little creek creatures. Where did the crayfish go in the flood?

A cow stood bawling on a little island of land surrounded by swirling water. A mud-smeared chicken clung to a board, its feathers plastered to its body. The chicken squawked every time the board bounced over a wave.

Then Rose heard a man's voice shouting. Across the flood, on the town side, some people were standing.

"I see them, too," said Mama. "It is the Cooleys! They must have come to see how we are."

They listened and Mr. Cooley shouted again. But they could not understand him over the sound of the flood. Now Rose could see Paul and George. She waved. Mama shouted back, "We're all right!"

But her voice was too small to reach. They all waved to each other, and then the Cooleys walked back to town.

On their way to the house, Rose spied something moving in a pile of leaves. She looked closer. It was a fallen nest, with four baby birds in it.

"Look, Mama!" Rose shouted. The baby birds' eyes were barely open. Their tiny naked heads wobbled. When Rose touched the nest, they stretched their scrawny necks and opened their delicate pink mouths to be fed.

"The poor things," said Mama. She looked about in the trees, but there was no mother bird to be seen. "She must have been killed, or flown off in the storm. They will die for certain if we leave them. Let's bring them inside and see if we can save them."

Mama carried the little nest carefully in both hands. In the house she took an old feed sack and rolled down the sides to make a cozy place to cuddle the nest in. Then she set it near the stove, where the little birds would stay warm.

"What can we feed them?" Rose asked.

"They are very young," said Mama. "I don't know if they are grown enough to eat worms and such. Let's try giving them cornmeal. I'll soften some in water."

Then Mama showed Rose how to feed the trembling chicks. She dipped a hollow stem of straw in the corn mush to pick up a little of it. She poked the stem in the mouth of one of the nestlings. The baby bird grabbed at the food greedily and gulped. The others made chattering noises and opened wide their trembling mouths.

Rose fed them all, again and again. She made sure to give each bird the same number of turns. After a long time they began to settle down. Then they huddled together and fell asleep. Mama carefully tucked the top of the feed bag closed to make it more cozy for them.

Rose and Mama spent the rest of the morning cleaning up. They moved the chicken coop into the barn. Then they pulled the tree limb off the garden fence and put the rails back in place. The rain stopped and the creek began to go down. The gray sky lightened.

Finally, just in time for dinner, Papa came riding back. He was soaked and muddy.

"It was pretty bad all right," he said. "We had to rescue a couple of Kinnebrew's cows from the creek. He lost three of his best milkers. They were standing under a tree when lightning struck it.

"But here's some good in it, anyway," he said, handing Mama a sack. "He butchered one of them and gave us a nice piece of beef."

There wasn't time to cook the beef for dinner. Mama said she would make a good stew of it for supper, with onions.

When Rose went to feed the nestlings she found one of them outside the nest, curled up in the corner of the feed bag. She touched it, but its fragile little body did not stir. It was dead. Rose's heart ached to see it.

"Perhaps it was injured," said Mama. "The others look quite healthy."

Rose fed the three nestlings again. Their tiny pinfeathers had dried out and stood up from their naked bodies. When she was done, she asked Mama if she could bury the poor dead bird.

"We'll do it together," Mama said.

She got the shovel and dug a little hole where Rose asked her to, under the big oak tree near the barn. Rose laid the tiny creature's body in the bottom. She crumbled up some muddy soil and covered it. She jabbed a stick in the ground, to mark the spot. Then they walked slowly back to the house.

Rose fed the three little birds many times, every chance she could, all afternoon in between helping Mama hoe the garden.

By supper the creek was almost back inside its banks. All in the woods and across the creek the land was covered with a layer of mud. Close by the creek the tree trunks wore necklaces of twigs and muddy grass above Rose's head, showing how high up the water had come. Across the valley some buzzards picked at a dead animal.

The dark clouds had moved on, and white ones filled their places. The lowering sun was a great, yellow eye sending a shaft of sunlight to fill the valley with a hazy glow. Then the light faded and a mist rose over the creek.

"We can thank our good fortune we didn't buy bottomland," said Papa over supper. The savory beef stew was delicious, the best meal they had eaten in a long time. "This may be a poor rocky ridge, but at least we know it'll never flood."

Rose fed the three baby birds every chance she could. Each morning she jumped out of bed and ran to the feed sack to see them. Each morning their pinfeathers had grown a little. Their voices were stronger, and they ate more hungrily. They could not seem to eat enough.

Sometimes the little birds stretched their tiny wings, like babies trying to walk for the first time. Rose put in little sticks for them to climb up on. She was so happy to see how well they were doing. Rose felt like a great mother bird. She would protect the babies and feed them until they were strong enough to fly away on their own.

But after three days, Rose noticed that the birds were not getting any stronger.

"Perhaps they need something different to eat," said Mama. "Why don't you catch some bugs and worms?"

Rose caught tiny grasshoppers and ants. She

dug worms up in the garden. But the nestlings did not know how to eat those things. The grasshoppers and ants crawled out of their mouths. The birds shook their heads to spit out the worms. Rose tried everything she could think of, bits of grass, oats, leftover beans.

But the little birds began to weaken. Their chattering hunger calls grew softer. More and more slowly they raised their open mouths to be fed. Rose became frantic with despair.

Then, one morning when she got up, she found the littlest one outside the nest, in the bag. It was barely breathing. She put it back in the nest, but it would not eat any of the cornmeal. By dinnertime, it was dead. Rose buried it under the oak tree, next to the first one.

That afternoon, when she went to feed the two that were left, one of them was outside the nest. She put it back in. An hour later, it was out again, but it would not open its mouth to eat. At suppertime, it was dead, too. Now there was just one nestling left, the largest.

Rose's spirits fell. She picked at her supper

and answered when spoken to only as much as she must. She wanted to do something to save the last little bird. She prayed for it to live. But her hope was melting away.

In the morning, Rose could not stifle a tiny sob when she looked inside the feed bag and saw the lifeless little body huddled in the corner.

"I'm sorry, Rose," Mama said, hugging her gently. "That is the nature of wild creatures sometimes. Only a mother bird can properly raise its young."

Rose knew Mama was right. But she could not stop thinking how small and weak those little birds had been, yet how bravely they had struggled to live. All the rest of that day her eyes stung with unshed tears.

Visiting Alva

Now every day was summery warm. The garden dried so quickly after the flood that the potatoes were saved from rotting. Weeds sprang up everywhere. The alfalfa and oats that Papa had planted in the ground between the apple saplings seemed to grow inches overnight. Even the oaks, the slowest of all the trees, began to unfurl their leaves. All the woods were bathed in a soft green light.

Papa rebuilt the henhouse. Then he plowed up a patch of new ground for corn. After it was harrowed smooth, he plowed long furrows with the mules. Then, when the oak leaves were the size of squirrel ears, Rose helped plant the corn in the furrows, four grains of corn together in each spot.

Each time she did it, she sang a ditty Mama had taught her:

"One for the blackbird,
One for the crow,
And that will leave
Just two to grow."

Sure enough, crows and other birds came to steal the corn as soon as they had dropped them in the furrows. Papa shot two crows and hung them from tree limbs to scare away other crows.

When all the corn had been planted, Papa hitched a log sideways behind the mules. The log pushed the soil along, covering up the kernels. But the crows still came to dig them out. Papa had to stay in the corn patch a long time, shouting and shooting at the thieving crows. Then at night the woods creatures came to steal the corn. But Fido barked and chased them away.

Abe and Swiney did not come to help very often now. They were busy helping Mr. Kinnebrew plant and hoe his crops.

When the corn was laid by, Rose had more time to play. She often went for walks in the woods with Alva. They hunted bobwhite nests along the fencerows. They were hard to find because the hen always covered her eggs with leaves when she was away. They counted thirteen of the tiny, pointed eggs in one nest.

They waded in Fry Creek, capturing crayfish and finding tiny Indian arrowheads along the banks. A frowning kingfisher dove into the water to catch fish. Rose stood in a small pool and watched the minnows going like flights of tiny arrows over her insteps. When their slithery bodies touched her skin, they tickled. Now and then a little belly flashed silver.

They tried to trick buzzards into coming down to earth. Rose and Alva flopped in the grass and lay as still as they could be.

"You cain't even twitch your little finger," said Alva. "They won't come down if they see we ain't dead. Buzzards only eat dead things."

They lay there in the grass the longest time. Rose opened her eyes just a little to peek now and then. The great birds soared and circled high above them in the sky. Each time she peeked, they were a little bit closer. But Rose couldn't be still so long. Ants crawled on her skin and made her itch and squirm. Right away those buzzards sailed off until they could see them no more.

Rose loved the woods. All the forest creatures were busy eating and nesting and raising their young. Beautiful flowers bloomed everywhere she looked. And now there were patches of blackberries to eat.

One morning Rose was helping Mama scrub the wash in the yard when Alva came tramping up the hill. She invited Rose to come to her house for dinner. Rose had never been to Alva's house. She was very excited and begged Mama to let her go.

"Very well," said Mama. "Remember your

manners, and thank Mrs. Stubbins. I will expect you home in time for evening chores."

The Stubbinses' house was a log house, too. But it was very big, with two whole floors of rooms. The first floor was two rooms, with an open-air hallway between them. Alva said that was the dogtrot. Two lanky, bony hunting dogs came loping out to greet them, panting and pleading with their eyes to have their heads scratched.

On the porch were a spinning wheel and a loom. Under an oak tree stood a quilting frame. The week's washing hung in the morning sunshine. There was line beyond line of sheets, overalls, shirts, underwear, and dresses.

Dozens of hens scratched in the yard. Geese walked statelily on the banks of a little spring branch. Ducks swam in a pond below the stone milkhouse. Rose could see pigs rooting in the woods above the spring. There was a summer kitchen, and a little smokehouse, and corncribs and cattle sheds, and a large ash hopper, and a pasture with a herd of beautiful Jersey cows, and horses and mules, too.

Rose had not known that Alva's family was so rich.

"Howdy, Rose," Mrs. Stubbins said heartily as she came out of the house. "We're right proud to welcome you. It's about time you was a-visiting. Alva's all the time bragging on you."

A wisp of gray hair fell across Mrs. Stubbins' smiling face. Rose liked her very much. She remembered meeting her last fall when all the neighbors came to help Papa build the barn.

Dinner was a merry feast. She sat next to Alva at a long table with all of Alva's brothers and sisters, six in all, her mama and papa, and a hired hand. Mrs. Stubbins had fried a big plate of chicken and another plate of ham. There were boiled potatoes and hominy and biscuits with butter to spread on them. Rose split open a biscuit and laid it crumbly side down in the fried-ham gravy. Then she carefully ate the biscuit halves, making four bites of each. She couldn't remember when she had eaten so well.

Mrs. Stubbins even gave Rose a big glass of delicious cold milk to drink.

On the other side of Rose from Alva sat Alva's oldest sister, Effie. Two of Alva's sisters were older than Alva, and one of her brothers was a grown-up man. Everyone was talking and laughing, all through dinner.

"How do you find it here in the Ozarks?" asked Effie.

"I like it very much, thank you," Rose said politely. "Except for snakes and chiggers."

Everyone laughed good-naturedly.

"Yep, we got ourselves a mess of snakes and other pests in these hills," said Mr. Stubbins, spearing another piece of ham with his fork. "You young 'uns got to watch out, running around barefoot all summer. Most snakes are harmless. But we got some that are right poisonous. Say, now, you ain't seen none of them hoop snakes about, have you?"

"No, sir," said Rose. "What kind of snake is that?"

Mr. Stubbins looked around the table with a twinkle in his eye. Effie giggled.

"Well, now," he said. "The hoop snake is one of God's strangest creatures. He only lives here in the Ozarks and not many folks has ever seed one.

"He climbs uphill like any sneaky old snake, slithering and sliding on the ground through the leaves and bushes." Mr. Stubbins wriggled his arm to make it slither like a snake.

"But when he wants to come back down the hill, he bites his tail in his mouth, makes himself into a wheel, and rolls down, just like a hoop. And fast as lightning, too."

"Oh, Emmett!" Mrs. Stubbins said. "Filling their heads with such nonsense."

"Oh, it's true, all right," Mr. Stubbins went on. "Now that old hoop snake is ornery. He likes to chase folks. The thing about it is, he's got a horn on his tail that is right sharp and mighty poisonous. Worse than a rattlesnake, or even a copperhead.

"His aim ain't too good, though. A hoop snake most always runs into a tree before he can hurt you. Then his horn gets stuck in the bark. And do you know what happens then?"

"What?" Rose said, her fork paused in midair.

"The leaves of that old tree curl right up, and in a few days, the tree dies."

Rose giggled uncertainly. Mrs. Stubbins rolled her eyes and got up to clear the dishes. Rose looked at Alva, but Alva was looking at her father with wondering eyes.

Then it was time for the grown-ups to go back to work.

"Thank you, Mrs. Stubbins," Rose said. "It was a very good dinner."

"Don't you even mention it," Mrs. Stubbins said. "You come any old time you please. And tell your ma and pa to come a-visiting of a day, too. There's always room at our table for good neighbors such as you'uns."

Rose began to pick up plates to help with the dishes.

"You ain't got to do that," said Alva. "My sisters do the washing up. Come on. I'll show you around our farm."

Rose thought Alva was very lucky to have big sisters to help with the chores. At home

Rose helped with everything. She was almost as busy as Mama, all day long.

Alva and Rose went into Mr. Stubbins' great barn and played with the baby calves. They let the calves suck their fingers. Alva showed Rose how to milk a cow, but Rose's hands weren't strong enough to make the milk come out.

They found one of the barn cats nursing her kittens in a hollow place in the hay. The mother cat was rust-colored, with a white spot around one of her eyes. She raised her head and blinked dreamily at Rose. The kittens were as tiny as mice. They paddled around with their little paws and sucked at their mother's stomach.

Rose picked one up and cuddled it in the palm of her hand. The kitten nosed between her fingers and mewed softly.

"When they get older, you can have one if you want, Rose," said Alva.

"Could I!" Rose shouted.

"Pa said we got too many cats," Alva said. "Which one you want?"

They all looked the same, with softly striped orange fur on their backs and velvety white fur on their bellies. Their tiny eyes were shut tight, and their tiny ears lay close to their heads. Their short, pointy tails stood straight up and trembled as they nursed. Only one had a black foot, and it was a little smaller than the rest.

"That one," said Rose. "I like that one because I can tell it from the others."

"I'll tell Pa and when he says it's old enough, you can come and take it," Alva said.

Rose clapped her hands with joy. "Thank you, Alva! Thank you so much."

They played away the rest of that afternoon. They watched Mr. Stubbins and the hired hand cutting hay and pitching it into stacks. They made a little dam in the branch of the spring and watched the water spiders darting on the water's surface. They made mud pies and left them to bake in the warm sun.

Alva noticed some bees drinking water from a rock. They tried to follow the bees when they flew away.

"If we can course them, we can find where the bee tree is," said Alva. "Then Pa can chop it down for the honey."

The bees took off one at a time, loaded down with water, and spiraled up into the air. But hard as they tried, Rose and Alva could not see where they flew off to.

Then it was time for Rose to go home. She went back to the barn to peek at her kitten one last time. She decided to name it Blackfoot.

Rose ran home, full of excitement. She ran through the Stubbinses' pasture, startling the cows chewing their cuds in the shade. She skimmed bushes and leaped over stumps. She laughed out loud when a frog she had startled *kerplunk*ed into Fry Creek.

But when she got close to home, she slowed down and walked. And she thought. It had been a wonderful day. She was very happy about her kitten. But a part of Rose felt hollow. She liked Alva's family. She had enjoyed all those people around to listen to and talk with.

Rose wished she had brothers and sisters to

play with. She wished she could visit Alva's house more often. She imagined how wonderful it must be to live at Alva's house, to be Alva and have so many wonderful things to do every day. Rose wished Mama and Papa had a cow, so she could have milk to drink, and butter for her bread.

Then she blushed hot with shame at her thoughts. But she could not stop from having them. A long time ago, when Mama and Papa had decided to move to Missouri from South Dakota, Mama had told Rose they would have sheep and cows again. Soon it would be a whole year since they had left Dakota.

Rose could see it would be a long while before Rocky Ridge Farm looked anything like Mr. Stubbins' wonderful farm. When the apple trees came into bearing they would have everything they ever wanted. But that was years and years away. Rose did not know how she could ever stand the wait.

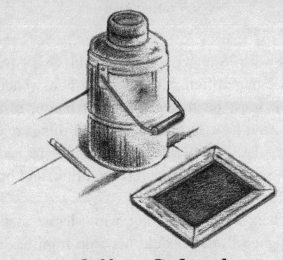

Off to School

Akitten?" Mama said in surprise. She stood over the kitchen table, ironing Rose's new dress, which she had just finished sewing up. "But where is it?"

"It's too little yet to leave its mother," said Rose. "It's orange and white, with a black foot. Its name is Blackfoot. I picked it."

"We certainly could use a good mouser," Mama said, changing the iron for a freshly hot one that sat on the stove. "When we get the crops in this fall we will need a cat to keep the rats and mice out of the corn and oats.

"There," she said, holding up the dress. "All

done. Let's put it on you so I can pin the hem."

Rose wriggled into the new blue and lavender gingham. The cloth was stiff with ironing and newness. Mama had tatted a lace collar for it.

"Your hands are soiled," Mama said. "Try to keep them away from the cloth." She stepped back to look at Rose, chin in hand. "That was a good choice you made. The blue matches your eyes. You look very pretty in it."

Mama's eyes shone as she looked. Rose fidgeted happily. She couldn't wait for a chance to wear it.

Rose stood on a chair so Mama could pin up the hem. Rose told her all about dinner at the Stubbinses', and about trying to milk the cow, and about hoop snakes.

"Are there really hoop snakes here?"

"I've never heard of one," said Mama. "I expect Mr. Stubbins was playing a little joke on you."

Rose was quiet for a moment as Mama worked her way around the hem. Then she asked, "Mama, can we have a baby brother, or a baby sister?"

Mama stopped pinning and looked at Rose with searching eyes. A shadow seemed to pass across her face, and then she sighed.

"I don't think so, sweetheart," she said softly. "Are you lonesome?"

"A little, sometimes," said Rose. "Why can't we have a baby? God brings babies to everyone else."

"You can take your dress off now," Mama said. Rose slipped back into her soft, cozy everyday dress and sat on the chair while Mama fed wood into the stove.

Finally Mama came and sat down at the table. "Do you remember, when you were a baby, when Papa and I were sick and you stayed with Grandma?"

"A little, I think," Rose said. She remembered living with Grandma.

"And do you remember right after that, the baby boy we had in South Dakota who died before we could give him his name?"

"Yes," Rose said in her smallest voice.

"Well, Papa and I wanted to have another baby, and we prayed for another baby. But I think that when I was sick, God decided we won't have one. We cannot do more than pray. After that, we must accept God's judgment. Do you understand?"

"I think so," said Rose. "But . . . why does God bring babies to some people and not to us?"

"God brought you, Rose. That was the greatest gift of all for Papa and me. To have you is enough, if that is His will. No one can know why God decides anything.

"And as for feeling lonesome, you won't be for long," Mama said. "School starts next week. Just think of the friends you'll make!"

Rose's mouth flew open to speak, but nothing came out. She had not thought about school for a long time. She had loved her school in South Dakota, but she didn't know if she would like it in Missouri.

The first day of school, Rose had to get up early to have time for all her chores. First she gathered stove wood from the woodpile and put it on the porch. Then she carried buckets of water from the spring for the horses and mules. She carried warmed water from the reservoir in the stove for the chickens.

She fed the chickens their mash and collected the eggs. Then she washed up and set the table. As soon as breakfast was done, she helped Mama wash the dishes.

Finally, she put on her new dress. The crisp new fabric felt smooth and cool against her warm skin. Mama buttoned up the back. Rose tried out the arms by hugging herself. The fabric didn't bind in the shoulders like her old dresses. Her body felt as free inside it as if she were wearing nothing at all.

Mama plaited Rose's hair tightly into two braids and bound the ends with thread. She tied on Rose's yellow hair ribbons. Then she went to the trunk and got out Rose's ruffled pinafore.

"Don't make a face, Rose," she said. "I know it covers up the cloth, but you must wear it to keep the dirt off. That dress must last until school finishes, at harvest time."

Then Mama took out of the trunk her old copy of *McGuffey's Third Eclectic Reader.* Mama had been a schoolteacher. While Rose was waiting to start school, Mama had taught the lessons at home using her old textbooks. Rose was all the way through the Third Reader and she knew it practically by heart.

Mama gave Rose her slate and a new slate pencil. She slipped the pencil in the pocket of the pinafore. Then she handed Rose an old molasses tin with a lid on it and a handle for carrying. That was her dinner pail.

"There's a surprise in it for you," Mama said. "Don't you peek or nibble before Teacher calls dinner. Promise?"

"I promise," said Rose. Now she was ready. Suddenly she saw that she really was going to school. Something churned in her stomach. "Mama, would you walk with me to school?"

"Why, Rose! You're a big grown-up girl now. I have chores to do, and Papa needs help in the woodlot. You know the way."

Rose sighed. "Can Fido come?"

"School is no place for a dog, and we need him here, to keep the snakes and hawks away from the chickens. Don't fret so, Rose. School will be fun, and Paul and George will be there. You best hurry now or you'll be late."

Mama kissed Rose and watched from the porch as she walked down the wagon tracks toward Fry Creek. Fido bounded alongside her, but Mama whistled for him to come back. Fido looked at Rose and cocked his head. Mama whistled again and he scampered away, back up the hill.

New Girl

R ose waded across the creek, holding up the hem of her dress so it wouldn't get wet. The cool water tingled on her bare feet and washed away the dust.

The footpath that went over Patterson's Hill started on the other side. Rose trudged up the hill past Williams Cave, where she had explored with Alva. They were going to play there again, but now that Rose was in school, she would have no time. The ringing of Papa's ax in the woodlot echoed in the valley. A train whistled loudly as it chugged into town.

The sun was already high, and the air was

shimmery warm. Rose pushed her sunbonnet back off her head. She could hear the voices of farmers as they went to work, shouting at their horses. Yellow daisies with black centers speckled the hillside as if someone had dusted it with yellow powder. Little white and yellow butterflies fluttered among the wildflowers.

Finally she reached the top of Patterson's Hill, from which she could see the back of the tall brick schoolhouse. Children were walking up the road from town. Other children were playing on the bare ground to the side. Three little girls rode a horse up to an open shed. Then they got down and tied up their horse with the other horses that were already hitched there. Rose looked for Paul and George, but she did not see them.

She walked slowly down the slope toward the school. Her heart pounded in her chest. Just then the bell began to ring and all the children raced toward the front door. Rose hurried not to be last.

Then she was in a crowd of children who were pushing, jostling, and laughing. At the head of the crowd, children were pouring through the big double doors. Rose caught a glimpse of Paul as he was swallowed up by the doors.

Finally Rose reached the entryway. A tall bald man with a long beard called out, "Fourth Readers upstairs to the left, Fifth Readers upstairs to the right. First and Second Readers to the left, please. No pushing. Third Readers to the right.

"You there, little girl in the plaid. What reader are you in?"

Rose stood just inside the door, not knowing which way to turn. A stream of children poured in around her.

"Which reader?" the man said again, impatiently. He tapped Rose on the shoulder.

Rose didn't know what to say. Then the man saw her book. He pointed, "Third Reader, to the right."

Rose walked through another door. A boy rushed past her, knocking her dinner pail to the floor. She picked it up and looked around. The room was full of double desks,

four rows of four desks. The floor was bright
yellow wood and shiny. The room smelled of
linseed oil.

There were many great tall windows all
around on three walls, and a large heating
stove against one wall. The opposite wall from
the stove was partly painted black. That was
the blackboard. All the other walls were
painted a pale sickly green.

On some of those walls were pictures of old
men with long beards. In between the pictures
were sayings, printed on large cards. One said,
"Kind Words Can Never Die," and another
said, "Be Diligent, Prompt, and Truthful."

Children were racing about the room, shouting and arguing over seats. Rose stood uncertainly next to the wall by the door. Then the
tall man with the beard was talking to her
again. "Have a seat, please. Put your dinner
pail on the shelf and sit anywhere on the girls'
side."

Rose put her dinner pail up and looked
around the room. It seemed every seat was
taken. Then she spotted an empty one at the

front, next to a girl with beautiful curly black hair falling in ringlets. She wore a lovely lawn dress and shiny black shoes. Rose liked to sit in the front in school, so she went to sit in that desk. But when she put her book and slate down on the desktop, the little girl turned and frowned at her.

"You can't sit here," she said quickly. "It's my friend's seat. She's coming in a minute."

Rose flushed hot. She stood in front of all those desks of strangers, not knowing what to do or where to go. Several children were staring at her. Two girls sitting together whispered to each other and pointed at her.

Finally Rose spied an empty seat in the back row. She almost ran down the aisle and quickly sat in it. She was relieved to be where no one could stare at her.

Then Rose looked at her seatmate. Her head was resting on her hands on the desk, her face turned the other way. Rose couldn't tell if she was resting or sleeping. Her faded brown calico dress had a large patch of gingham sewn on the front. Her brown hair fell limp and unbraided over her shoulders. Her feet were dirty. Then she sniffled loudly.

"Hello," Rose said politely. "My name is Rose Wilder."

The little girl looked at Rose blankly with weary eyes.

"I'm tired," she said. Then she wiped her nose with the back of her hand and laid her head down again.

Rose's heart began to sink. There was no sign of Paul or George. They were older, so they would be upstairs in the Fourth Reader.

Now the teacher began to speak.

"My name is Professor Kay," the man said. He wrote his name on the blackboard in chalk. "You may wonder why I have such a long beard. Well, it is to cover my shirt so I do not have to wear a tie."

There were giggles all around the room. Rose could not tell if Professor Kay was making a joke or not.

Then Teacher took the roll. He called out many names. Rose had seen some of the last names on stores in town. "Blanche Coday," he called out. Rose remembered Coday's Drugs.

The girl with the beautiful black hair called out, "Present, sir." Her seatmate was very pretty, too. Her blond hair hung in a silky braid down her back. Her white dimity dress had a butterfly pattern on it. A gold bracelet hung from her wrist. She was looking around the room with bright, curious eyes and whispering to Blanche.

"Quiet in the classroom," Professor Kay said. "Maude Reynolds, Hattie Talbott, Tarah Tarbutton, Clella Rippee, Ida Goss, Oscar Hensley, Harry Carnall . . ." And everyone answered, "Present, sir," or "Here."

Rose listened anxiously so she wouldn't miss her turn. One by one, the students answered to their names. Her throat grew so choked with expecting to speak that she could hardly breathe. Finally, all the names were called, including Irene Strong, the snuffling girl sitting next to Rose. All the names had been called except Rose's.

"Is there any scholar here whose name I did not call?"

Rose raised her hand.

"Stand up, please," Professor Kay said. He pointed a long stick at her. Everyone in the room turned to look at Rose. Her neck blazed hot under all those eyes. "What is your name, please?"

"Rose Wilder," Rose whispered.

"Speak up. I can't hear you." Titters rippled around the room.

Rose said her name again.

"Very well," Professor Kay said, writing it down. "Be seated."

Rose hated being stared at, and laughed at. Irene Strong smelled like a barnyard. She snorted and sniffled.

The desk seat was too tall. Rose's legs ached from dangling. The room was stifling hot. A trickle of sweat ran down the back of her neck.

Rose had never had a teacher who was a man. She had loved Miss Barrow, her teacher in South Dakota. Miss Barrow was pretty and she had a beautiful voice; she liked to lead the class in singing. Rose had loved her classes there, and she had had many school friends to play with.

Now Rose had only one thought in her mind, to run out of that school and all the way home. She would go home and she would never come back. But she did not budge from her seat. She was too shy to run away.

Then the lessons began with recitations. Professor Kay called on the boys first.

"Harry Carnall, recite, please, the first paragraph of 'George's Feast.'"

A boy in overalls stood up and read slowly from his reader, "George's mother was very poor. 'Stead of havin' bright blazin' fahrs in winter, she had nothin' to burn . . ."

"Ing!" Professor Kay barked. "No-*thing*." He stood up and wrote on the blackboard, *having*, *blazing*, and *nothing*. The chalk jabbed and scratched angrily as he wrote. After *nothing* he wrote ten times, *ing*, *ing*, *ing*.

He turned around, folded his arms across his chest, and glared at Harry Carnall.

Harry giggled nervously and looked around at the other boys. Professor Kay just stared at him. Finally Harry said, "What's the *ing*, *ing*, *ing* doin' up thar a whole passel of times?"

"I am glad you asked that question," Professor Kay said. Then he wrote out what Harry had said on the blackboard, with spaces between the words.

"I wrote the *ing* up there ten times so you won't forget it. I have hardly heard anyone pronounce *ing* since I came to this school last winter. We are going to learn it now. Let us all say *ing* together, ten times."

Everyone sang out a chorus of *ing*s. All those *ing*s together sounded like a pondful of spring peepers. Rose kept her mouth shut. She did not need to learn how to pronounce *ing*. The lesson was stupid.

"Now," Professor Kay said. "The word is *fire*, not *far*. And it is *there*, not *thar*."

Everyone took turns reciting. One boy could not read at all.

"Do you at least know your ABC's?" Professor Kay asked.

"Heck no!" the boy shouted out in amazement. "I ain't been here but a few minutes."

185

The room erupted in laughter. Even Professor Kay cracked a small smile. Then he sent the boy to the First Reader across the hall.

Rose grew bored waiting her turn. She was the last to recite.

"Recite, please, the first two paragraphs of 'Johnny's First Snowstorm.'"

Rose knew her whole book almost by heart. She recited easily:

> *"Johnny Reed was a little boy who never had seen a snowstorm till he was six years old. Before this, he had lived in a warm country, where the sun shines down on beautiful orange groves, and fields always sweet with flowers.*
>
> *"But now he had come to visit his grandmother, who lived where the snow falls in winter. Johnny was standing at the window when the snow came down."*

"Very well done," Professor Kay said. "Please be seated."

Rose knew she should have been pleased

with Teacher's praise, but she didn't care. She knew all of her Third Reader. She had even read the Fourth and Fifth Reader as well. She had read *The Adventures of Robinson Crusoe*, and she often read *The Chicago Interocean,* a newspaper Papa brought home.

So she sat there, legs aching, prickly hot, listening to Irene's horrid snuffling, looking at the ugly green walls, and watching Professor Kay. He tipped back in his chair against the blackboard. He looked out over the class through steel-framed spectacles. He carried a long stick that he poked down the back of his soiled shirt to scratch himself.

Finally Professor Kay rang a tiny bell that he kept on his desk. That meant to put books away. He rang it a second time for everyone to stand up. The third time he rang it was dismissal.

Rose could hardly wait to see Paul and George. She raced outside with all the other children and waited by the doors. Paul came clomping noisily down the stairs with two other boys. His face lit up in a wonderful way when he saw Rose. His bright smile was like the sun coming up.

"Hey, Rose!" he shouted. "Finally came to school, huh?"

"Yes," said Rose cheerfully. "But I don't like it very much. I wish I could be upstairs where you are."

"It's not so bad," he said. "At least you don't have to stay home and do chores. And then you can play at recess and dinnertime."

Just then another boy cried out, "Two-cornered cat and one my bat!"

All the boys raced around to the boys' side of the schoolhouse to play a game.

"See you later!" Paul shouted. Then he dashed off to follow them.

George came racing out of the schoolhouse. He shouted hello to Rose and ran off to play two-cornered cat.

Rose was by herself. She watched four boys carrying water buckets down to the spring at the bottom of the hill. A group of town girls in pretty dresses, including Blanche Coday, were playing house with some rocks. But they did not invite Rose to join them and she was too shy to ask.

Some other children were playing crack the whip. But Rose's spirits were so low, she did not feel like joining. She looked longingly at the crest of the hill that stood between her and home.

Recess was over in fifteen minutes. The bell rang and all the children crowded through the door again. Inside they pushed and shoved to get a drink of water from the bucket before they had to sit down. Two boys wrestled over the dipper, knocking it to the floor.

Rose waited until everyone else had gotten a drink. But when she looked in the bucket, there was not enough water left to get even a dipperful.

The rest of the morning dragged on. Professor Kay wrote on the blackboard, *Exercise in verbs. Insert words in the following sentences: The dog_____at the cat. The horse_____the wagon.*

Rose stared out the window at the trees rustling in the breeze. A bluebird flashed past the windows. Rose wondered what Alva was doing today. Probably she was helping her papa bring in the hay, or playing with the kittens, or just about anything that was more fun than sitting in that stuffy schoolroom.

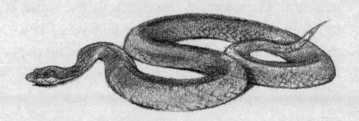

Afternoon Lessons

At noon, Paul and George went back to the hotel to eat dinner with their mama and papa. The children who stayed at school gathered in groups of friends, or sisters and brothers. Rose ate by herself under a tree at the edge of the playground.

In her molasses tin she found two pieces of brown bread with bacon fat spread on them, a boiled potato, and a dried-apple turnover. That was Mama's surprise.

Rose ate the turnover first. The sweet, crisp taste melted in her mouth. Eating it made her feel a bit better. Then she slowly ate her bread and the potato. Two girls who were twins sat near her. They were dressed exactly the same, in sprigged green calico. Their hair was fixed exactly the same, arranged in a tidy bun on the tops of their heads. Out of their large tin they each took a piece of fried chicken and a biscuit.

"You're a new girl, aren't you?" one of the twins said. "Come and eat with us. We like to meet new girls."

"Thank you," Rose said gratefully. She picked up her things and sat down next to the twins.

"My name is Dora," one of the girls said. "This is my sister, Cora. We're the Hibbard twins. Have you heard of us? Everybody knows us in town. What's your name?"

"Rose Wilder," said Rose.

"You aren't in the Fourth Reader," said Dora.

"I'm in the Third Reader," Rose said. "This my first day in school. I used to live in South Dakota."

"I know where that is," Cora said proudly.

"It's very far. All the way north. Almost to Canada."

"Are Paul and George in your reader?" Rose asked. "Their mama and papa brought them here from South Dakota, too."

"Paul and George? Are they brothers who live in the Mansfield Hotel?" asked Dora.

Rose nodded.

"We don't like George very well," said Cora. Dora nodded in agreement.

"He is in our class," said Dora. "He teases the girls by putting bugs down their backs. Boys are pests, anyway."

"And he pulls their braids," Cora added. Rose thought Dora and Cora were like one person, split in half. Even their voices were exactly the same. She wondered how anyone could tell them apart.

"Would you like a piece of our chicken?" Cora asked. "We have lots."

She held out a crisp, golden-brown chicken leg. Rose's mouth watered at the sight of it. She wanted to accept. She loved chicken and Mama only made it sometimes, when a hen got too old to lay. But she thought it might be impolite to take food from strangers.

"No, thank you. I'm full."

"We love school very much," said Dora. "The first day is so much fun. We like to see our friends again, and everyone is so excited."

"We hate it when school ends," Dora said. "There's nothing to do until it starts again."

"I liked school in South Dakota, but I don't like it very much here," said Rose. "The girls are not very friendly. I mean, except for you. And the teacher is a man. I like a woman teacher better."

"So do we!" Dora said cheerfully. "We like Miss Pimberton so very much."

Rose chatted with the Hibbard twins until they had finished their dinner. Then they all joined some other girls who were playing cat and mouse.

All the children held hands in a circle. One person was the cat and another was the mouse. The mouse started in the middle of the circle. The cat prowled around the outside. Then the cat chased the mouse, darting into the circle under clasped hands. The mouse dashed out and the cat chased her around and through the circle until the mouse was tagged.

Then the mouse became the cat, and it was someone else's turn to be the mouse.

Rose liked cat and mouse. The sound of other children giggling and shouting, and the excitement of all that running and shrieking, cheered her up. When it was her turn to be mouse, her legs rejoiced to be running and free. Soon she was laughing as hard as anyone else.

When the bell rang for afternoon books, Rose went to say good-bye to Cora and Dora, but she hesitated.

"Good-bye, um . . ."

"I'm Cora," Cora helped. "Would you like to know how to tell us apart?"

"Oh, Cora," Dora moaned, making a sour face.

"Just look at Dora's left ear. See, she has a fawn's ear."

Dora's ear was pointed. But the twins' names were so much alike, Rose thought she would never get them straight. On her way back to her seat, Rose wondered what it would be like to have a sister who looked and sounded exactly like her. Twins were lucky, she decided. They always had a best friend to play with.

When Rose sat down in her seat, the two girls sitting in front of her were whispering excitedly and looking at one of the boys. Rose looked at the boys' section. There was a great deal of giggling and snorting among them, but Rose could not tell what it was about.

Professor Kay had just rung the bell to take up books when Harry Carnall jumped to his feet.

"*Ow!*" he shouted. Then he began jumping and writhing in the strangest way, as if he were having a fit. All the children burst out in noisy laughter.

"What's the meaning of this?" Professor Kay demanded.

Harry didn't answer. He was jumping about and digging his hands in his pockets, trying to pull something out of them. Suddenly, from the bottom of his pant leg, a blacksnake slithered out and raced across the floor.

The room erupted in shrieks and shouting and stamping as everyone tried to frighten the snake away or stomp on it. Rose stood on her seat. She would never shriek at a snake, but she didn't want one crawling on her.

Finally Teacher took his stick and picked up the snake. He threw it out the window.

"Harry Carnall," he said in a terrible voice. "I will not tolerate such disruptions in my classroom. Step to the front."

Harry's face was scared and flushed, but he could not stop himself from giggling.

"Hold out your hand," Professor Kay said sternly. Harry held out a hand. Professor Kay took it and bent the fingers back. Then he whipped the open palm of Harry's hand with his stick five times. Harry winced in pain.

Finally, Teacher went to the blackboard and drew a small circle in chalk.

"You will stand here until recess with your nose pressed on the board in the middle of this circle," he said. "And you will remain in at recess."

No one could concentrate on lessons with Harry standing there, his face pasted to the blackboard. When Professor Kay rang the bell to put down books, Harry was finally allowed to go to his desk. His nose was red and there was a damp spot on the blackboard where it had been.

After recess was spelling. Professor Kay drew a long, straight chalk mark on the floor at the front of the classroom. Everyone stood on it in a line, in alphabetical order, facing Professor Kay. No one's name started with an "X" or a "Y" or a "Z," so Rose's name was last. She must start at the foot of the line. Then Teacher called out words and each student took a turn spelling, beginning with the person at the head of the line.

Spelling was Rose's best exercise, and she knew all the words.

"*Frequently,*" Professor Kay said when it was her turn.

"*Frequently,*" Rose repeated. "F-r-e *fre*, q-u-e-n-t *quent, frequent;* l-y *ly, frequently.*"

Rose felt a tingle of excitement every time

she got a word someone had misspelled and she could move up one place in line. Soon she had spelled down two students, and she was third from the foot.

All afternoon they spelled. Rose moved up the line, closer and closer to the head, closer to Blanche Coday, the girl who wouldn't let Rose sit with her. Blanche was a good speller, and she had spelled down the two boys who were ahead of her.

Finally, Rose stood next to Blanche and Rose was only one word away from being the best speller in the class that day. Her stomach quivered, her hands were cold, and her palms were damp. She wanted more than anything to spell down Blanche Coday.

But Blanche was a good speller, too. Every word Professor Kay gave her she spelled correctly: *curious, purpose, material, cautiously.* Every time she got one right, Blanche looked at Rose smugly. But every word Professor Kay gave Rose, Rose spelled correctly as well: *reminded, including, constructed.*

The next time it was Blanche's turn, Professor Kay said, "*Chiefly*."

Rose knew that word, too. She crossed her fingers behind her back.

"*Chiefly*," Blanche said, tossing her head so her curls shook. "C-h-e-i-f *chief*." Rose trembled with joy. "L-y *ly*; *chiefly*."

It was everything Rose could do to keep still. She knew by heart the rule "'I' before 'e,' except after 'c.'" Blanche had got it wrong! Rose's whole body poised to pounce on that word.

"Wrong," said Professor Kay. "Next."

Blanche shot a hard, pinched look at Rose.

"*Chiefly*," Rose said with confidence. "C-h-i-e-f *chief*, l-y *ly*, *chiefly*."

"Very good," said Professor Kay. He wrote Rose's name on a corner of the blackboard and put a mark next to it. That was a headmark, for Rose had gotten to the head of the line by turning down all the other scholars.

"That will be all for today. Class is dismissed."

Everyone scrambled to leave. Rose picked up her book, her slate, and her molasses tin, and bounded out of school. Girls like Blanche might laugh at her, but she could beat any of them in spelling. She flew home, running down Patterson's Hill and splashing carelessly across Fry Creek.

Fido ran down the wagon track to meet her, barking with joy. Rose was never so happy to see him, and Mama, too, when she came to the kitchen door, drying her hands on her apron.

So much had happened that day that Rose didn't know where to start the telling.

"First things first," Mama said. "Change your dress and gather in some kindling for the stove. Then you can help Papa feed and water the horses. You can tell us all about school when we sit down to eat."

Mama untied the sash of Rose's pinafore and carefully pulled Rose's dress off over her head. Then she hung it up behind the curtain in the corner, so the wrinkles would hang out for tomorrow.

The whole house seemed to smile at Rose, glad she was home. The warm, moist smell of fresh bread hung in the air. Salt pork sizzled cheerfully on the new nickel-plated stove. Mama whistled as she rattled a stove lid to check the fire. Rose could hear the mules braying in the barn as Papa fed them their supper.

When Rose finished her after-school chores, she washed her hands and face and set the table. Finally, Papa came in to wash up. It was wonderful to be home.

She told Mama and Papa that the town girls in her reader were very pretty but they were rude. Her seatmate was awful, she smelled bad, and her nose ran all the time. She didn't like Professor Kay very well, either.

"He's dirty and he's the stupidest teacher in the world," Rose complained. She knew it was wicked to say, but all her feelings from that day just came tumbling out before she could stop them. "And he gives the stupidest lessons. 'The dog barked at the cat.'"

"That's enough of such talk, Rose," Mama said firmly. "Besides, people aren't stupid. They are just more or less foolish."

"He is more and more foolish," Rose said.

Papa chuckled, but then stopped when he saw that Mama was not smiling.

Then Rose told Mama and Papa that the schoolroom walls were painted an ugly green that gave her a strange feeling in her insides. The walls made her sick.

"You are just imagining it," said Mama. "You must not be so silly. Besides, you would not be looking at the walls if you were studying like a good girl."

"But the lessons are dull," Rose said. "I know them all. I know all the spelling words, too. I made head in spelling."

"That's very good," Mama said. "I'm proud of you."

But Rose did not feel proud. It had been too easy.

They sat down to supper as the sun was setting. A cooling breeze came in the doorway. A mockingbird that had nested in a tree by the log house began its long, sweet song from the chimney top. The sound floated down the chimney and echoed inside. Katydids and tree toads began their nightly chorus, shattering the quiet with their shrilling songs. From Fry Creek came the chuckling songs of frogs.

"You must have seen Paul and George," Papa said. "How are they doing?"

"I saw them," said Rose. "But they are in the Fourth Reader, on the second floor. At recess they play with the boys. They go to the hotel for dinner."

As they ate supper, Rose told Mama and Papa about the Hibbard twins and about Harry Carnall and the snake. Papa laughed so hard he nearly choked on his food.

Then Rose fell silent in thought. Mama did not understand how unhappy she was in school. Rose could not bear another day sitting next to Irene, staring at those walls, and watching Professor Kay scratch himself. She simply couldn't.

When they were done eating and Papa sat back to light his pipe, Rose finally screwed up her courage to ask, "Do I have to go back? Can't I stay home and study my lessons here, like before?"

"Why, Rose, it's only the first day!" Mama

said, getting up to clear the dishes. "You mustn't give up so easily. In time the other students will catch up to you, you will make some friends, and then it will be more fun."

Rose frowned.

"Don't pout," said Mama. "What must be done is best done cheerfully."

In Trouble

Rose woke the next morning with a terrible feeling of dread. She would have begged Mama to let her stay home, but she knew it would not change a thing.

She dawdled so long on the way to school that she was the last to take her seat. Irene did not speak to her again. At recess she watched Paul and George and the other boys playing. Morning recitation dragged on, and Rose stared out the window.

She listened to the birds singing and watched cloud shadows moving across the hillside. She thought about Alva, and about Blackfoot. She wondered if the little kitten had opened its eyes yet. Rose wished she were a bird. She would fly out the window, over Patterson's Hill, up Fry Creek, right to Alva's barn, where she would sit in the hay and play with her kitten.

Rose was startled from her thoughts when Irene nudged her in the ribs.

"Rose Wilder!" Professor Kay called out impatiently. "I said, please rise and recite."

Rose sprang to her feet, knocking her reader to the floor with a thud. Blanche chortled and some of the other children giggled. Rose's cheeks burned hot.

She picked up her book. "I . . . I'm sorry," she said. "I lost my place."

"Please recite the first three paragraphs on page thirty-one, 'The Beaver.'"

Rose found her place and recited those paragraphs perfectly.

Noon finally came. Rose dashed outside and wolfed her dinner down in nothing flat. When she was done she put her tin back on the shelf in the classroom. Then Rose left school. She couldn't fly to Alva's, but she could run.

She ran all the way to the Stubbinses' farm. She must hurry to have time enough to get back before afternoon books. Alva was just coming out of her house from dinner.

"How come you ain't in school?" Alva asked.

"I am," said Rose. "I just wanted to see Blackfoot."

"Come on, then," Alva said. "Their little eyes are open now."

Sure enough, all the kittens' eyes were wide and shining and looking curiously at everything. They had grown so in just a few days. Now they played with one another, gnawing each other's ears and tails, pouncing, and kicking with their tiny back feet. Rose and Alva laughed at how comical they were.

Rose picked up Blackfoot. He climbed up her pinafore onto her shoulder. He sniffed tiny breaths that tickled in her ear, and batted at her hair ribbon. Then he mewed softly to get down.

"Oh, Alva," Rose said. "I hate school so."

"I'm glad my ma and pa don't make me go to no school," said Alva. "My pa says you don't need no schooling to know how to milk cows and hoe corn. I just know I couldn't sit in those old seats for a minute."

Then they left the kittens and walked out into the yard to get a drink at the spring.

"Look, Rose!" Alva shouted. "The bees are back drinking water. Let's follow them and see if we can course the nest."

"I don't think I ought to," said Rose. "I might be late for afternoon books."

"We won't go far," Alva insisted. "Come on, there goes one now."

A bee had taken off from a moss-covered rock. It circled around and around until it was high in the air. Then it took straight off in a beeline into the trees, flying slowly.

Alva took off running and Rose followed. "I can still see it!" Alva shouted. They ran through the woods, a long way. Rose could never see the bee, but Alva kept shouting, "There it is! Hurry up, Rose!"

But then she lost sight of it. "It don't matter

anyway," Alva said. "'A hive in May is worth a load of hay, but a hive in July ain't worth a fly.'"

On the way back they passed by the horse pasture. They watched two colts racing each other back and forth across the field. Then they hunted quail nests along the fence. They found a blackberry patch. Alva took a stick and beat the bushes first, to scare away snakes. Then they plucked and ate all the ripe berries they could find.

Rose remembered school, but she was sure she still had time to get back for afternoon books. She had not heard the bell, and it wasn't so far if she ran.

Along the spring branch they hunted crayfish. Then they built a dam and watched a little pond form behind it. Brilliant blue dragonflies hovered darting to catch bugs.

Finally Rose said she had better go. She ran all the way back to school. The sun seemed much lower in the sky now. She had better hurry not to be late. When she got to the top of Patterson's Hill, Rose gasped. The schoolyard was empty! She slowed to a walk, catching her breath. Then she noticed that there were no horses tethered in the shed. Her stomach flip-flopped.

The last thing she noticed made her heart skip a beat. There was a wagon standing by the front of the school. She recognized Pet and May, Papa's horses.

A great weight settled around Rose's shoulders. She walked very slowly down the hill, around the front of the school. She climbed the steps, one at a time. Her feet were as heavy as stones.

As she got to the top of the stairs, she heard Mama's voice, and Professor Kay's.

Then she stood in the schoolroom doorway. Mama was sitting in a desk with her back to the door. Papa stood next to her. Professor Kay looked up at Rose from his desk. He nodded toward her and looked at Mama with raised eyebrows. Mama turned and looked at Rose. Her mouth was tight and her eyes glared fiercely.

Professor Kay cleared his throat. "I best be going," he said. "I expect you have the matter in hand now."

Then he left without another word.

"Where have you been?" Mama asked sternly. Her voice had never had such a hard edge.

Rose could think of nothing to say. She stared at the floor.

"I asked you a question," Mama said. "You weren't in school all afternoon, and Teacher dismissed class an hour ago. Papa and I have been worried sick. *Where have you been?*"

Rose flinched.

"I went to Alva's," Rose said meekly. "I'm sorry, Mama. I only wanted to see the kitten. I didn't know it would be so long."

Mama said, "To think, you could have been lying hurt somewhere, and Papa and I with no idea where to begin to look. I can't imagine where you got it into your head . . ."

"Now, Bess," Papa interrupted. "There's no need to get too stoked up. She's here now, safe and sound. Just some childish foolishness. But you mustn't ever do anything like that again, Rose."

"Yes, Papa," Rose said softly.

Mama said, "We have told Professor Kay to keep you in during recess and dinner as many days as he sees fit, until you have learned your lesson. You must obey him the same as you obey Papa and me."

"Yes, Mama," Rose said.

The silence on the ride home crashed in Rose's ears. She wanted to cry, but she didn't dare. She hated causing Mama and Papa to worry.

Every day for the rest of that week Professor Kay kept Rose inside during recess and dinner. At first it was torture to be still and listen to the high, light voices of the other children playing outside.

But Professor Kay chatted pleasantly with Rose while they ate their dinners.

"You are a very good student, Rose," Professor Kay said. "I don't blame you much for being bored. By rights, you ought to be in the Fourth Reader. Your mother taught you well."

"Thank you," Rose said, trying not to speak with her mouth full. She munched on a carrot that Mama had put in her lunch. Raw carrots were Rose's favorite vegetable.

"I expect it takes some getting used to, coming into these hills for the first time," said Professor Kay. "A lot of these folks have never been out of the Ozarks. Just a few miles from here there are people who have never seen a railroad train."

"A man told Papa that once," said Rose. "When we drove here last summer. The man said people here had never seen an organ or a train."

Professor Kay's beard crumpled into a smile. "I'll tell you a story. Once there was a young fellow who lived back in the hills who had never seen a train. He had to go to town for the first time, and it was several days' journey. One night he slept on the ground, and along around daybreak he woke up to a tremendous roaring sound. He looked up and saw the biggest thing he had ever seen come running out of a hole in the hillside, near where he was sleeping.

"He was scared. He took off and ran away. He just ran and ran. Finally he saw a woods-man splitting rails. He stopped to catch his breath, and the woodsman asked him what he was running from.

"After the fellow got his wind back, he told the woodsman that he had just seen the worst thing in his life. It was some kind of beast, huge, that was snorting and raging something fierce. The thing was black and it had one great big shining eye and fire and smoke were coming out of its head. He said it just came tearing out of its den in a hillside, and it was making a terrible racket and letting out a great yell now and then."

Rose giggled.

"Now that woodsman told this young fellow that he'd seen a train, is all. He told him, 'It won't hurt you. You can even ride on it.' And this hill boy said, 'It'll have to catch me first.'"

Rose burst out laughing. Professor Kay chuckled, too.

Then Rose had a new thought.

"Could I go into the Fourth Reader, Professor Kay? My friends are in that class. Paul and George. I promise I would be good and study hard to keep up."

"I am sure you would, and I wish I could say yes," Professor Kay said. "But Miss Pimberton's room is full and you are a bit young for her class. I'll tell you what, though. There is a library of books in her room that have been donated to the school. If you wish, you may pick one out to read. Would you like that?"

"Yes, sir," Rose said. "I would like it very much. Thank you."

When they were done eating and Rose had put away her tin, she walked upstairs with Professor Kay to Miss Pimberton's room. In the corner was a bookcase with four shelves. The bottom part was where the erasers and the boxes of chalk were kept. Above it were three shelves behind glass doors. Two of the shelves were almost full of books.

Professor Kay said Rose could look through those books. He opened the glass doors so she could pull them out and see if she would like to borrow one.

Rose had never seen so many books. There were books of poems by Alfred, Lord Tennyson and William Clement Scott; Prescott's

History of the Conquest of Mexico and *History of the Conquest of Peru*, *The Green Mountain Boys*, and *John Halifax, Gentleman*, and another true book, the biggest of all: *Ancient, Medieval and Modern History*, full of beautiful colored maps and pictures.

There were many storybooks, too: *Afloat in the Forest*, *Five Little Peppers and How They Grew*, *Five Little Peppers Grown Up*, and important-sounding books: *Sense and Sensibility*, *Pride and Prejudice*, and *The House of the Seven Gables*.

Rose loved the feel of the cloth covers and the rich weight of the books in her hands. She couldn't decide on just one. She wanted to read them all, to learn the secrets hidden in all those hundreds of pages of words. Finally she picked a big book called *The Leatherstocking Tales*. It had been written by a man named James Fenimore Cooper many years before. Rose picked it because she liked the title. Professor Kay said it was a book of stories about the beginnings of America.

At noon the next day Rose sat at her desk,

ate her dinner as quickly as she could, and read. She began at the beginning. The first part was called *The Pioneers*.

She read about Leatherstocking, a nickname for an old man called Natty Bumppo who lived in New York State and who hunted deer in the wild forests. Rose did not understand some of it, and there were quite a few words she had to ask Professor Kay to explain.

But the more Rose read, the more she wanted to read. It was very pleasant to sit quietly in the empty classroom. In no time at all she was carried away from school. She forgot about the green walls and about Irene. Instead, she was tramping through the winter snows of New York many years ago, hunting deer with a smoothbore rifle, and wearing a deerskin coat with the hair still on.

When the bell rang for afternoon lessons, she hated to put it down. Rose thought the people in books were more real than the people she saw every day.

In the afternoon each day there was spelling. Every day Rose started at the foot and ended at the head. She always turned down Blanche Coday. But even though they ended up standing next to each other, Blanche did not speak to Rose, and Rose was too shy to speak to Blanche.

On Friday, Professor Kay let Rose take the book home with her. On Saturday night and Sunday afternoon, Mama read aloud from it to Rose and Papa. Mama liked that book very much.

"It reminds me of when I was a child, growing up in the Big Woods of Wisconsin," she said. "Your grandpa used to hunt deer and bear, just as Natty Bumppo did."

On Monday Rose took *The Leatherstocking Tales* back to school. Her punishment was ended and she could go out with the other children. But she would still read it. She propped herself up against a tree at the edge of the schoolyard and opened the book on her knees.

But before she could sit down to read, Professor Kay gave her a chore. He asked Rose to clean the erasers. That was a special chore that he only gave to the best students. Rose was surprised that after she had been disobedient he would give her a special chore. But she was even more surprised when Professor Kay picked Blanche Coday to help her.

At dinnertime, she and Blanche took two erasers each and walked quietly to the edge of the playground. They clapped the erasers together to get all the chalk dust out. A fog of chalk dust floated on the breeze, making them both sneeze. They must clap and clap those erasers until no more dust came out of them.

They did not speak a word to each other. Rose could not think of anything pleasant to say to Blanche, and Blanche turned her back to Rose.

Rose stole as many looks as she dared at Blanche's beautiful lawn dress, her shimmering, curled black hair, her shoes and stockings. Rose hated to wear shoes, but all dressed up that way, Blanche was simply beautiful. And she seemed to wear a different dress every day of the week. Rose could not imagine owning as many school dresses as there were days in the week. She had one dress, and it must last the whole school term, until fall.

Blanche's father was rich. Rose had heard some other children say it. He owned Coday's Drug Store. Rose wondered what it must be like to be rich. She would have liked to own any one of Blanche's dresses, and she would like to eat chicken every day, and have butter on her bread instead of bacon fat.

The next day, as they were clapping the chalk dust out of the erasers, Blanche startled Rose by asking her in a haughty voice, "Where are you from? You aren't from around here. Anyone can see that. You don't talk like girls from around here."

"My mama and papa brought me here from South Dakota," Rose said. "We drove last summer in a covered wagon all the way."

Blanche clapped her erasers a few more times. Then she said, "You haven't been in school here before. How did you learn so many spelling words?"

"My mama taught me," said Rose. She did not like the tone of Blanche's voice, but she tried to be polite anyway. "She was a school-teacher once. I like to read, too. I learned many words from reading books."

"Well, anyone can see that plain as day," Blanche said tartly. "It's all you do, is read and stare out the window and be teacher's pet. But don't think we can be friends just because you are so smart. After all, you're a country girl."

With that, Blanche flounced off to return her erasers. Rose's face stung as though it had been slapped. She stared hard after Blanche, boiling with anger. Alva was right, Rose thought. Town girls are stuck up.

Rose decided then and there that she would never, ever let Blanche Coday spell her down.

Summer

Every day in spelling Rose turned down Blanche and ended up at the head of the line. Every day Professor Kay put a headmark next to Rose's name on the blackboard. And Rose remembered each time her promise to herself and studied her spelling harder.

Irene took sick and stopped coming to school. Irene's older sister said Irene had caught diphtheria. The word echoed in Rose's mind like a thunderclap. That was the terrible illness Mama and Papa had once had.

The doctor had been to visit Irene, and now

the rest of her family could not leave their house because they were quarantined. Only Irene's sister could go out to school and to town on errands. But she said she must sleep in the barn, so she would not catch it, too.

Rose felt sorry for Irene, but she was glad to have the seat all to herself now.

Summer flowed on, slow, lazy, and stifling hot. Specks of dust hung in the still air, catching the sunlight and shimmering in the heat. The hot weather pressed down like an iron pot lid.

It was prickly and sticky sitting inside the classroom, even with all the windows opened. Everyone was glad to dash outside at dinnertime and sit in the cool shade of a tree to eat. Most days Rose ate by herself and read. Paul or George visited with her sometimes. Sometimes she played cat and mouse, or sat and talked with other students. She liked Cora and Dora best of all.

But Rose did not make a best friend at school. Many children had brothers and sisters in school. The families ate and often played together. The town girls snubbed her. Rose did not want to be friends with other country girls like Irene whose mothers sent them to school unwashed in shabby dresses. And the boys played rough games and kept to themselves. Rose did not fit in anywhere.

But she was mostly content. She had grown to like Professor Kay. She enjoyed watching Paul and the older boys playing two-cornered cat. And Rose had been an only child all her life. She was used to pleasing herself.

At home, the whole farm was growing. The garden was rows and rows of different shades of green. Mama liked to keep a neat garden. She and Rose hoed and chopped weeds every other day until the soil was smooth and soft and clean between the lush columns of leaves. There were radishes, lettuce, onions, and carrots. But the carrots did not grow like any carrots they had seen. They were crooked and thin from struggling to reach down through the stony soil. The tomatoes had blossomed, and now there were shiny pale-green tomatoes hanging from thin stems.

Baby melons clung to the melon vines, and potato leaves sprouted all along their heaped rows.

The corn had sprung up almost overnight. It was growing taller every day, unfurling bright new leaves that fluttered in the breeze like ribbons. Already the stalks reached Rose's waist. She could almost watch them grow, the corn was shooting up so fast.

In the same soil with the corn Papa had planted the pole beans. The thin tendrils of their stems trailed along the ground, crawling straight to the corn. Then they hugged the cornstalks and began to climb them. The cornstalks were the poles. Before they picked the corn in the fall, the beans would be ready to harvest. That was a way to get two crops out of one piece of ground. Rose wondered how the beans knew to climb the cornstalks.

In the orchard the young apple trees were filling in with new growth. Slender, bright green fingers reached out from the end of each gray branch and twig. Papa brought home wagonloads of wood ashes from town and spread some around each tree. The ashes would sweeten the soil and keep away wood-eating bugs that might hurt the trees.

One Sunday Alva came by, carrying a sack that meowed loudly. She opened it and out jumped Blackfoot. He shook himself, blinked in the bright light, and rubbed, curving, against Rose's leg.

"He remembers me!" she cried. Blackfoot was even more beautiful than she recalled. And he had grown so big. His short, straight tail had become long and wavy.

When Fido came to sniff at him, the kitten batted the dog's nose playfully. Fido gave a short surprised bark that sent Blackfoot skittering behind Rose. But in a moment he came back out, sat down, and licked his paw, keeping his bright eyes on Fido. Soon after that they became friends and even played together.

It was often too hot to sleep at night, even with all the windows open. Some nights Rose's legs itched so from chigger bites that even if she could fall asleep, the burning and itching kept her awake. And it was noisy, too. Katydids, crickets, frogs, and other night creatures made such a clamor in the dark woods that when Mama read aloud she almost had to shout to be heard. Only in the wee hours before daybreak did all those creatures finally go to sleep.

One night at supper Papa said, "It's too blamed hot for cutting wood. The crops are laid by, not much hoeing and plowing to be done. Why don't we gather up some folks and throw ourselves a picnic?"

"That would be lovely," said Mama. "After all, we were too busy with the corn to go to town on Fourth of July. We could all do with a change of scene. Do you think the Cooleys would come?"

"Don't see why not," said Papa. "I'll ask them when I'm in town tomorrow."

"Perhaps we could ask the Kinnebrews as well," Mama suggested. "We haven't all met them yet."

In a day it was decided. The three families would meet on the Ava Road south of town and drive down to Bryant Creek.

The morning of the picnic they woke up in the false dawn, hurriedly did their chores, ate a cold breakfast, and loaded the wagon. Papa pitched a pile of hay in the back to sit on and for the horses to munch. The picnic food was packed in a basket with a clean white towel tucked over it. A jug of sweetened ginger water sat under the wagon seat.

Rose gave Fido's head a good scratching and explained to him that he must stay behind and guard the farm. He whimpered in disappointment.

Then they were off in the first gray light of dawn. They met the Kinnebrews in their wagon and the Cooleys driving the hotel hack. There were many shouts of hello, and they drove off into the fresh morning with Papa's wagon in the lead. The wagon track twisted and turned through the hills under a canopy of branches heavy with leaves. Rose tingled with excitement to be going somewhere different, and to have a day away from school.

It had been a whole year since they drove to Missouri from South Dakota. That had been a great adventure, and now that it was summer again, Rose remembered the wonderful, new things they had seen along the way. Going somewhere made her feel like singing. She hummed, "Oh Susanna."

Right away Mama began whistling it, and then they were all singing as the sun peered over a ridge and lit the tops of the trees.

The wagon rattled past many small farms along the way, with log houses and barns tucked away in little hollows. Horses and cows munching the dew-fresh grass lazily watched them pass. Farmers waved from their corn patches. They passed small white churches and a schoolhouse. Rose could see children inside studying their lessons. They stopped often to let the horses rest and have a drink from the little streams and springs they crossed all along the way.

Nits and horse flies buzzed around the team. Papa had to keep the lines tight in case they suddenly bolted from being bitten and tried to run away.

Finally, when Rose was getting fidgety and

the air was turning muggy, they came to a wide stream, bigger than Wolf Creek. That was Bryant Creek.

They set themselves up on a gravel bar, right next to the water. Rose helped Paul and George gather wood for a fire. Mama and Mrs. Cooley hung an old sheet between two trees for a private place to change into the old dresses they had brought for swimming.

Mr. and Mrs. Kinnebrew had brought two big watermelons for everyone to eat at dinner. Rose's mouth watered just looking at them. Their two sons, Coley and Claude, carried them to the creek's edge and set them in a quiet pool to chill. They weighted them down with stones to keep the watermelons from floating away. Mr. Kinnebrew scolded the boys to quit fighting over how to pile up the rocks.

"I'm going to wear you two out if you don't behave," Mr. Kinnebrew said irritably. "It's bad enough we're missing a day's work without having to listen to you two scrapping all the time. Now give a hand unhitching the team."

There were three Kinnebrew children in all. Coley was a big boy, a year older than Paul, who was eleven. Then there was Ernestine, who was nine, the same age as George. Claude was the baby of their family. He was seven, a year younger than Rose. Rose had seen all of them at school, but they were in different classrooms for lessons.

Mrs. Kinnebrew was a very proper-looking lady. She wore a beautiful lawn dress, and her hair was pinned up in a tight bun. She carried a dainty white parasol, with ruffles around the edges.

"I don't like to wear a bonnet if I don't have to," she told Mama. "It's too hot in this country."

"You came here from Illinois, didn't you?" Mama asked.

"Yes, and a prosperous little town it was, too," Mrs. Kinnebrew said, puffing up like a hen that had just laid an egg. "I often wonder what Mr. Kinnebrew could have been thinking of when he dragged us all down here. This is lovely country from nature's point of view, of course. But it is a mighty poor excuse for a place to try to dig out a living."

"The ground's a bit thin and stony," agreed Papa. "But you can't beat it for fuel and the best water that ever flowed out of Mother Earth."

"And the people are so friendly," Mrs. Cooley said. "So neighborly and helpful."

"I suppose, although they are somewhat poor-folksy, don't you think?" said Mrs. Kinnebrew, smoothing the front of her dress. "And there are so many pests and varmints in the timber that try to destroy our livestock. We have had a wolf carry off two of our pigs. And last fall the rats killed eleven of my young chickens, and two turkeys, too."

"A wolf?" Mama said, casting a worried glance at Papa. "I hadn't heard of that. Why, your place isn't a mile away from ours."

Then Coley chimed in, "They call this Missouri but they ought to call it the state of Misery, right, Ma?"

"I wish you would stop making fun of this fine country," Mr. Kinnebrew said. "We should use our own judgment and push ahead and not let discouraging words alter our course.

"I never saw a place yet that wouldn't raise a fair crop if farmed right, and I'm going to give this country a good tryout before I give up. I'll work till doomsday but what I'll succeed. I know we can make a good living if we don't lose our ambition."

"It is never easy to start over," said Mama. "We are doing it ourselves."

Finally, when the wagons were unloaded, the horses tied up in the shade with buckets of water to drink, and the food assembled for dinner, the children were free to play.

Picnic

First they threw rocks into the creek. Claude said he wanted to scare away all the cottonmouth snakes in the creek so they could swim.

"I hate snakes," he said. "There are too many snakes around here."

"You're afraid of everything," Coley scoffed. He was tall and blond. A shock of his blond hair covered his forehead and shook as he hurled a skipping stone. It skipped almost all the way across the creek. That stone somehow went into the water and popped right out again, time after time. Rose had never seen anything like it. She tried to make stones skip, but they only plopped and sank.

"You think there's a bear behind every tree," Coley said with a smirk. "Just waiting to jump out and eat you. You're afraid of your own shadow."

Claude turned red-faced and punched Coley in the side. "I am not either," he shouted. In a second they were on the ground wrestling. But Claude could not possibly win against Coley. Coley was a big grown-up boy. He sat on Claude's chest and pinned Claude's arms with his knees. Then he tickled the inside of Claude's nose with a grass stem until Claude cried, "Uncle!"

"I'm tired of you two fighting all the time," Ernestine huffed. "I'm going to go sit with Mother and help with dinner."

Rose thought the Kinnebrews were not a very happy family.

The creek was very wide. They had stopped in a place where two streams flowed together. In the middle where the streams met was a point of stony land. It was like an island, or the bow of a boat. The water made a rushing sound as it ran around it.

Rose wanted to explore the island. But the current looked swift, and in the middle of the creek was a large pool. It was dark there, too deep to see the bottom even through the clear water. The creek looked so fresh and inviting that Rose wanted to jump right in and get her whole skin wet. But Mama said she must stay dry until after they ate, so she wouldn't have to change twice.

But even if she had been allowed to, Rose did not know how to swim.

"Stay close to the bank," Mama called out, as if she had heard Rose's thoughts. So Rose only waded along the creek bank, hunting crayfish and Indian arrowheads with Paul and George and talking about school.

Then they chased grasshoppers to fish with after dinner. Every minute Claude was hollering, "There's a snake!" But there never were any. He was just imagining them.

It was very hard to catch grasshoppers. They were the same color green as the grass.

The only way was to scare them up and then watch one flutter away to see where it landed.

Then Rose crept up behind that grasshopper. When she was close enough, she swooped her hand down to grab the grass stem where the grasshopper clung. She tried many times before she finally caught one. The grasshopper kicked and fought in her fist, giving Rose's palm a queer tickly feeling.

They put all the grasshoppers they caught in a sack.

When dinner was ready they all gathered together to eat. The men had dragged logs near the fire to sit on. In the trees around them, cicadas shrilled in the warmth of the day. Their raspy sounds rose and fell, like knives being sharpened on lopsided grindstones.

There were pickles and steaming potatoes that had been roasting in the fire. Mama had brought hard-boiled eggs. Mrs. Cooley had made a big batch of biscuits with snowy white insides, and she passed them around. Everyone admired and enjoyed them.

"It's nothing, really," Mrs. Cooley said.

"When you feed a hotel full of guests you are accustomed to making big batches."

"How is it, living in town?" Mrs. Kinnebrew asked. "It must certainly be more civilized than living on a farm in the middle of nowhere. I suppose you see many interesting people in the hotel."

"Yes, but we are too busy to visit," said Mrs. Cooley. "It seems all we do is work. And the noise! When it isn't the trains and the trade coming into town, there are fights that break out at the saloon. And just the other day some farmers tipped over one of the boxcars on the siding."

"Whatever for?" Mr. Kinnebrew asked.

"It was parked right where the tracks cross the road," Mr. Cooley said. "The town asked the railroad to move it three times, but they never did. Folks got tired of bouncing their wagons over the rails and ruining their wheels. I guess some fellows took it in their own hands to show the railroad company a lesson."

"That reminds me of the story about Mr. Arnold's hog," said Mama with a twinkle in her eye. Rose perked right up. She had never heard this story.

"It was in Walnut Grove, Minnesota, one fall at butchering time when a freight train ran over Mr. Arnold's fat hog about halfway up the hill east of town. He couldn't save the meat, but he rendered the fat into soap.

"Mr. Arnold tried to get the railroad people to pay him for the hog, as they should have. But they refused. He had no money to go into a lawsuit and the railroad knew it.

"So one day, before the freight came through, he went and soaped up the rails. He smeared the soap all up and down the track. When the train came along its wheels spun and spun on the slippery rails and it couldn't pull up the grade. The train crew used up all the sand they were carrying and had to get out and throw dirt on the tracks to get going again.

"Every day after that, the freight train never could get up the grade without sand and trouble. The passenger train went through all right, but when the freight came, it slipped and fell behind schedule.

"The railroad people were suspicious, but they never could catch Mr. Arnold in the act. Finally, the railroad sent a man out to Arnold's one day and paid him cash money for his hog. Sure enough, the very next day the freight went through without any trouble.

"After that, Mr. Arnold bragged in town that he'd given most of that hog to the railroad company, bit by bit on the rails. But he had a little of the soap left over, so he figured he had beat them out of that much of it anyway."

Even Mrs. Kinnebrew laughed when Mama finished.

When they had eaten their dinner, they cut and ate the sweating watermelons. The melons were deliciously sweet, and the children competed to see who could spit the seeds farthest.

Finally Rose and Ernestine and Mama and Mrs. Cooley changed into their oldest calico dresses to go swimming. Mrs. Kinnebrew sat on a log and watched. The men and boys went swimming right in their overalls.

Papa swam far out into the deep water. He

dove down and disappeared with a splash. Rose held her breath. She waited and waited for Papa to come up again. No one could stay under water so long. Rose was just about to scream for Mama when Papa's head popped out of the water, far away downstream from where he had vanished.

Rose wanted to swim with Papa and go under the water. She wanted to see what it was like down there. She walked deeper and deeper into the water.

Rose squatted down until the water came to her chin. She felt herself rising up, light as a leaf. Her dress blossomed up around her. Then it got wet and sank, sticking to her all over. Her whole skin drank up the refreshing coolness.

"Don't go in any farther," Mama said.

Suddenly, Papa's dripping wet head rose up out of the water, right in front of her. He laughed a great laugh that echoed from the creek bank.

"Will you take me in the deep water, please, Papa?" Rose begged. "I want to disappear under the water."

Papa laughed again. "I think you need a lesson first," he said. "Give me your hands."

Papa took Rose's hands in his own and gently pulled her away from the shallow water. Rose's feet lifted right off the gravel bottom. Then she was floating like an angel. The bank looked very far away. The water flowed over her skin like a cool breeze.

"Now kick your feet," said Papa. "I'll hold you up, and you kick with your feet." Papa towed her into the deep water. Rose kicked as hard as she could. Papa towed her around and around.

She stopped kicking to see if she could touch bottom. But there was nothing there, nothing solid to touch. Only deep dark water. And it was colder down there, too. The coldness on her feet scared Rose. If Papa let go, she would sink down and down in that cold darkness and nothing could stop her.

"Keep kicking," said Papa. His smiling face was always in front of her, going backward. "Now I'm going to let go of your hands. You must paddle with your hands, as if you are climbing up a slope, or crawling. And keep kicking, too."

Then Papa let go. Rose paddled as fast and hard as she could. But she could not make her hands and feet go at the same time. When she paddled with her hands, her feet stopped. When she kicked with her feet, her hands stopped. Then Rose felt herself sinking. Her head went into the dark water and she gasped, swallowing a great mouthful of water.

In an instant, she felt Papa's hands lift her up. Rose sputtered and coughed until she could catch her breath.

"Now you know what can happen if you go into deep water without knowing how to swim," Papa said. "I think that is enough for now." He towed Rose back to the shallow water.

"Can we do it again, Papa?" Rose begged.

Papa laughed. "I have a better idea," he said. "You can hold on to that old fence rail over there. It will float and you can paddle around. But only so long as I'm watching."

Rose kicked around the creek after that, her arms draped over the fence rail. Sometimes Paul or George would grab on to it, too. They were a ship, sailing on the ocean. The current carried them downstream to a wide shallow place. Then they got out and pushed the fence rail back upstream along the bank and floated down again.

All afternoon they played. There were horseshoes to throw. They cut cane and fished for a while. But the fish would not come to the grasshoppers. Papa said it was so hot even the fish weren't hungry.

Coley and Paul played lap jack. They locked their left arms together by hooking their elbows. Then they swatted each other with switches they held in their right hands.

Coley was taller than Paul and he landed the best blows. Rose laughed to see them both trying to get away and hit each other at the same time. Soon their shoulders were covered with red welts, but the boys were laughing loudly.

They stopped when Mr. Kinnebrew scolded Coley for waking him up from his nap in the wagon. "How is a poor farmer to get a little rest with all this commotion!"

Finally all the play was drained out of Rose.

She lay down on her back on a wide, flat stone that was big enough for her whole body. The heat from the stone warmed her wet dress. She looked up into the sky, at piles of fat, white clouds floating above the trees.

She gazed at the shapes the clouds had made. They were always changing, but she could never actually see them change. She stared at one cloud, hard as she could. It was a great tower of whipped cream. She stared at the folds and bulges and nothing changed. Then she looked away for a moment. When she looked back, the shapes had begun to dissolve, ruffled by the wind like tousled hair.

Each time Rose looked away, the cloud had changed, tearing itself apart in shreds and dissolving into a new shape.

She turned over on her stomach and yawned. She stretched her arms out to the side and felt the warmth of the rock soaking into her body. That rock was alive. The heat of its life was flowing into Rose. She hugged it. Rose felt as if she were hugging the whole beautiful living earth and the earth was hugging her back.

She loved that rock and she loved that summery day. The warmth on her skin, the rich odor of the damp soil, the peaceful chuckling of the water, the lazy buzzing of insects, and the murmur of grown-up voices all filled her with peace. She could not possibly have an unhappy thought. It seemed to Rose that summer could soothe every care and heal every hurt.

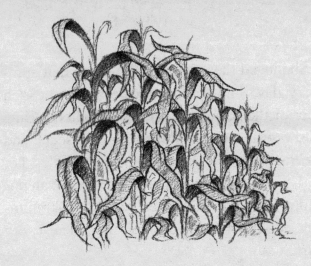

Jungle of Green

They went picnicking two more times that summer, with Abe and Swiney to Wolf Creek. By the last time Rose had learned how to use her hands and feet together. Now she could swim in deep water. But she never did unless Papa was with her. Deep water still frightened her.

At school, Rose stayed at the head of the line in spelling, although often it was very close. Blanche was a good speller and she only missed the hardest words. Some days when Rose sat reading her book at dinner, she noticed Blanche studying her reader.

Rose learned her times tables as well. Professor Kay had taught the scholars how to sing the tables to the notes of "Yankee Doodle Dandy." On the way home Rose skipped to the beat and sang to herself, "Five times five is twenty five, and five times six is thirty, five times seven is thirty-five, and five times eight is forty."

One morning, before they took up books, Professor Kay stood before the class with a grave look on his face.

"I have an announcement to make which is very sad," he said. All the rustling and fidgeting in the room stopped. Every head snapped to attention as if they were all connected to Professor Kay by strings he had pulled.

"Irene Strong, who has been out of school these many weeks with diphtheria, has crossed to that other shore from which no traveler returns." One of the girls choked out, "Oh!" All around Rose children were looking at each other with open mouths and big, scared eyes.

Rose was confused. She leaned across the

aisle toward the boy sitting in the next row. "What did he say?" she whispered.

"She's gone and died," the boy hissed. "Irene's died."

"We will bow our heads now for a minute of silent prayer," said Professor Kay.

Rose was too stunned to think of praying. Her mind skittered about like a water spider. The only person she had ever known who had died was her little brother. But she had been only a baby then herself. She didn't really remember anything at all.

Irene had not been Rose's friend, but she had sat right next to Rose. Rose remembered how unkind she had been to Irene in her thoughts. She remembered how she had complained to herself about Irene's sniffling and shabbiness. Rose's whole body blazed with shame.

Then she had a new thought. What if she caught diphtheria? Would she die? Did it hurt to die? And what would become of Mama and Papa if Rose died? They would never have other children. Mama had said so. Who would help on the farm?

The thought of Mama and Papa alone was the most unbearable of all. Tears flooded her eyes and fell from Rose's bowed face, splashing on her folded hands. She fought back a sob. She could hear some of the other children muttering their prayers. Someone was sniffling.

Professor Kay did not need to raise his voice or punish anyone all the rest of that week. Rose wished she could move her seat, but all the other seats were full. She could not help thinking of poor Irene whenever she looked at the empty spot beside her.

The days flew by and summer grew old and dusty.

"Seems as though it has been weeks since we had a good rain, Manly," Mama said at breakfast one morning. "The garden soil has just about dried all through. It's cracking at the surface. If this keeps up much longer, I'll need to haul water."

"It's the rocky soil, Bess," said Papa. "It's too thin and porous to hold the moisture. It drains right away. But the weather evens up in the end. This is the best time for a dry spell, just before the harvest. Too wet and the corn could go moldy."

"Yes, and the dryness has kept the bugs down in the garden," Mama said thoughtfully. "I just can't help remembering all those years of heartbreaking drought and stunted crops in South Dakota. How many times the weather robbed all our hard work at the last minute."

Papa only nodded in agreement as he got up to go cut wood in the woodlot. There wasn't anything to be said about the terrible hardships of the prairie that had not been said a hundred times before.

The corn had grown very tall, and now it was heavy with the ripening ears. The beans had climbed up the stalks. Bulging pods hung everywhere. In between the rows, here and there, pumpkins grew. Soon they would have their first harvest from the new farm.

The flat, empty field Rose had helped plant with the pitiful little seeds in the spring had grown into a wonderful, mysterious place to explore. In it Rose found another world, far away from Rocky Ridge Farm, where she could lose herself without being afraid. Sometimes she liked to go into the corn patch and just sit and listen. It was a jungle of green, rustling with life. The waxy corn leaves shone in the sunshine. In the early morning, sparkling beads of dew clung to the leaves and trickled down into their dark throats.

Rose liked to walk down the shady rows between the stalks, listening to the whispering leaves and imagining that she was Natty Bumppo stalking wild animals in the deep, dark forest, or Robinson Crusoe exploring a deserted island. Sometimes when Swiney came they played hide-and-seek there. Fido and Blackfoot tagged along as well.

September came, and the last day of the summer school session drew near. Professor Kay announced on Monday that there would be a special spelldown on Friday after supper. Then there would be no more school until after harvest time, in December.

"Each classroom will have its own spelldown," Professor Kay explained. "Your mothers and fathers are invited to come and attend and see how well you are all getting along. There will be refreshments after and a prize for the winner. I advise you scholars to study well if you are to make a good account of yourselves before your families."

Rose was terribly excited and jittery all that week. Every time she thought about the spelldown, her insides quivered. She knew she could win. She had gotten almost all the headmarks in the class. But Blanche was getting better and better. She had gotten three headmarks when Rose made mistakes. All that week during recess and dinnertime, Rose stole anxious glances at Blanche studying in her reader.

After dinner on Friday there was no spelldown. Instead the students scrubbed the whole classroom until it shone. Rose helped wash the blackboard and sweep the floor. The windows were washed as well.

Then they all cut pieces of red, white, and blue paper into strips. They glued the strips into little rings and strung the rings together to make paper chains. Professor Kay stood on a chair and tacked the paper chains around the windows.

When the classroom was spotless and decorated, school was dismissed. Rose dashed home to do her chores and get ready. Mama had washed and ironed Rose's best calico. After supper they all washed up, got dressed, and walked to school.

When they got to the top of Patterson's Hill, Rose and Mama slipped on the stockings and shoes they had been carrying as the sun began to melt into a puddle of gold. Rose swallowed hard as they walked down the hill into the schoolyard.

Spelldown

The schoolyard was teeming with wagons and horses. People were streaming in from every direction, dressed up and in a festive, friendly mood.

At the door of Rose's classroom, Professor Kay greeted Mama and Papa and invited them inside.

"Good to see you folks again," he said. "Come on in and have a seat."

School looked very different with all those grown-ups milling about. Rose spied Blanche, standing with her parents. Blanche's best dress was even more beautiful than the dresses she wore every day. It was made of red serge trimmed with satin that shimmered in the light of the setting sun.

Finally Professor Kay asked all the parents to be seated. There weren't enough seats to go around, so many people had to stand along the walls. Lanterns were lit, and the air filled with the smell of coal oil smoke. Rose took her place at the foot of the line of scholars standing against the wall. The grown-ups looked funny sitting in the tiny seats, their knees crowded. They looked like giant children. Professor Kay rose to speak. He had dressed up as well. He was even wearing a tie.

"We are honored to have all the parents here this evening," he said as the scuffling and murmuring faded away. A baby cried out in the back and everyone giggled nervously. Rose could hear voices and feet moving upstairs in the other classrooms, where the older children were having their own contests and recitations.

"We will begin the program with a few words from one of our patrons, Mr. Elliot Hoover, who, being the town livery man, a member of the school board, and the father of one of our students, hardly needs introducing."

Mr. Hoover stood and talked for a long time. Everyone was very polite and listened solemnly. But his voice was a blur to Rose. She was thinking of words she might have to spell.

"We are proud of our scholars studying so diligently . . ." Mr. Hoover said.

"*Diligently*," Rose thought. "D-i-l-i *dili*, g-e-n-t *gent*, l-y *ly*. *Diligently*."

Mr. Hoover was a tall, thin man with a drooping mustache. His enormous Adam's apple stuck far out of his neck and bobbed up and down so much when he talked that it was all Rose could do to keep from staring at it.

Mr. Hoover droned on and on until Rose's legs ached from not bending. He talked about the school board's business, how much money was spent and how much was collected in taxes. Finally he looked at the scholars and said, "In conclusion, students, the town is pleased to provide you this opportunity to improve the shining hours of your youth, just as I did with mine. For I was once only a schoolboy like any of you, and look at me now."

Professor Kay led the audience in singing a song. Then there were recitations by two other students. Finally, the spelldown began.

"We will begin with two warm-up rounds," Professor Kay said. He sat down at his desk, pulled his gold watch from his vest pocket, and opened the spelling book.

The words in the warm-up rounds were easy, and Rose began to relax. Anyone could spell them—*kettle*, *beyond*, *mouse*. Rose looked at Mama and Papa and smiled.

Then the real spelldown began and the words got harder, and trickier.

"*Counsel*," pronounced Oscar Walters, the boy standing ahead of Rose. "C-o-u-n *coun*, s-i-l *sil. Counsel*."

"I'm sorry. That is wrong," Professor Kay said. Oscar shrugged and hung his head as he shuffled out of line to go sit with his mother and father. Rose liked starting out at the foot of the line. It gave her heart to hear other students making mistakes.

"Next."

"*Counsel*," Rose said confidently. "C-o-u-n *coun*, s-e-l *sel. Counsel*."

Papa winked at her. Mama smiled.

One by one, the students were spelled down and left the line to join their families. The line became ragged, like an old comb with teeth missing.

"*Constructed*," Blanche said slowly, as if she were confused. "C-o-n *con*, s-t-r-u . . ." She hesitated. Rose's heart fluttered. "C *struc*, t-e-d *ted. Constructed*," Blanche said with a little sigh.

"That's my girl," a man in the audience whispered loudly. It was Blanche's father, Mr. Coday. Blanche blushed brightly and stared down at her shiny black shoes.

Soon there were only three students standing, Rose, Blanche, and a redheaded boy named Oscar Hensley.

"*Sheaves*," Professor Kay said.

"*Sheaves*," Oscar repeated. "S-h-e-e-v-e-s, *sheaves*."

"I'm sorry, Oscar. That is wrong. Well, ladies and gentlemen," Professor Kay said,

"we are down to the two best spellers in the Third Reader. May the better of them win."

Rose felt every eye in the room on her. Blanche got the first word. Then Rose, then Blanche. Blanche spelled every one correctly: *pendulum*, *conquer*, *locomotive*, *portrait*. Each time she spelled so slowly that Rose was certain she was about to make a mistake. But she never did.

On and on they spelled, into the evening. Clapping and a commotion upstairs in one of the other rooms told Rose that some of the other spelldowns had ended. Her mouth had grown dry, and she desperately wanted to sit down.

"*Occasion*," Professor Kay said.

"*Occasion*," Rose repeated. She opened her mouth to spell when suddenly her mind went blank. "*Occasion*," she said again. Her thoughts raced. One "c" or two; one "s" or two? Her chest tightened and she felt herself gasping for breath.

She looked at Mama and Papa. Papa was twirling his mustache. Mama twisted her handkerchief in her hands.

"*Occasion*," she said a third time. All the shuffling and fidgeting in the room came to a stop. Everyone was staring at Rose. A chair creaked in the awful silence as someone leaned forward to hear better.

Rose was too terrified to speak. She didn't know which it was, two "c"'s or two "s"'s! Or two "c"'s *and* two "s"'s. Which was it?

Professor Kay cleared his throat. Rose's heart began to pound in her ears.

"Do you wish me to repeat the word and define it?" Professor Kay said gently.

"No," Rose croaked. She must try, even if she got it wrong. She closed her eyes tight, trying to see that word in her mind.

"*Occasion*," she said slowly. "O-c *oc* . . . c-a *ca*, s-i-o-n *sion*. *Occasion*."

"Good girl!" Papa called out rather loudly. Nervous laughter broke out in the room. Mama's hand flew to her mouth.

"Correct," Professor Kay said. Rose let out a shivery sigh.

There were four more rounds of perfect

spelling. Then Professor Kay gave Blanche the word *precipice*.

"*Precipice*," Blanche said slowly. Rose thought she saw Blanche tremble, but she wasn't sure.

"P-r-e *pre*, c-i *ci*, p-i . . . s-e *pice. Precipice*."

"Oh!" someone in the audience cried out. Papa slapped his hand on the desktop. Mama turned and shushed him.

At first Rose did not understand what had happened. Then Professor Kay said, "Wrong."

Rose could hardly believe her ears. She knew how to spell that word. Blanche had got it wrong!

Professor Kay looked at Rose. "'Precipice,'" he said.

"*Precipice*," said Rose. "P-r-e *pre*, c-i *ci*, p-i . . . c-e *pice. Precipice*."

The room erupted in a swirl of shouting and clapping and confusion. Suddenly everyone was on his feet, moving about and talking. Oscar clapped Rose on the back as he ran past. Professor Kay was shouting something about lemonade on the second floor. Then Mama and Papa came pushing through the crowd up to Rose. Papa gave her a big hug. Mama smiled her biggest smile.

Rose realized with a shock that she had actually won the spelldown.

"That's our smart girl," Papa said. "You did it! You beat 'em all hollow."

"We are very proud of you," said Mama.

Then Professor Kay was there. "Very well done, young lady," he said. "Here is your prize, well deserved I must say, close as it was."

He held out to Rose a book. She took it in her hands. It was heavy and thickly covered with plush. The plush was deep red, soft as moss. Inscribed on the cover in shiny gold lettering was the word "Autographs."

Inside that book all the pages were blank, with beautiful curlicue borders printed in pale blue. Mama said it was an album, for friends and loved ones to write little sayings and poems in. It was a place to keep memories of good friends and special times.

"Every girl must have one," said Mama. "I did."

Rose looked at all those blank pages. How would she ever fill them up? She didn't know very many people she could ask to write in it. But she trembled with excitement to think of those empty pages filling up with words no one had thought of yet.

Rose was jumping with joy inside her skin, but she said politely, "Thank you, Professor Kay." She ran her hands over the velvety cover. It was so smooth and silky it could have been alive.

But when Rose spotted Blanche across the room, her joy began to melt into something else. Blanche stood slump-shouldered with her face buried in her mother's bosom. Her father was patting her on the head and saying something to her.

While Mama and Papa talked to Professor Kay over her head, Rose stared at Blanche's heaving back. The more she looked, the worse Rose felt. Yet she could not tear her eyes away. She thought about how close she herself had come to losing.

Rose looked at her beautiful new album,

and then back at Blanche. She tried to think of something to do. Blanche had been unkind to Rose, but Rose did not hate her. She didn't really ever hate anybody. She just thought they were more or less foolish, as Mama said.

But Rose did hate to be the cause of Blanche's tears. She thought and stared and thought some more. Then, in a flash, she knew what she must do.

Rose walked across the schoolroom, right up to Blanche's family.

"Why, hello there, young lady," said Mr. Coday. "You really gave us quite a show here tonight."

Blanche turned from her mother to look at Rose. Her cheeks were damp and her face was blotched. Her reddened eyes flashed and her mouth pinched itself into a frown.

"Please don't cry," said Rose. "I'm sorry you lost. I almost lost first. I couldn't remember if *occasion* has one 'c' or two. I only guessed. I was just lucky."

Blanche's frown softened. She looked down at the autograph album in Rose's hands.

"Professor Kay gave me this for winning. It isn't fair to give only one prize when we are such equally good spellers," said Rose. "We can share it, if you like."

Rose held out the album.

Blanche stared at it with disbelieving eyes.

"Well, isn't that something?" Mrs. Coday said. Then she nudged Blanche with her elbow. "Have you lost your tongue?" she said sharply.

"Thank you," Blanche murmured.

"That's a fine gesture, young lady," Mr. Coday said quickly. "You are an example to us all. But a memory album, now, that isn't a thing easily shared. Besides, you did win it, fair and square, luck or no."

"Yes," Blanche said, the storm clearing from her face. "It is your prize. You must keep it for yourself. But thank you. You are very nice to offer."

"We can take turns keeping it," said Rose.

"It wouldn't be right," said Blanche. "Thank you very much."

Rose thought for a moment. Then she had another idea.

"Will you write in it, then?" Rose asked. "Since we are both the best spellers, I would like you to be the first one to write in it."

"I . . . I wouldn't know what to write," Blanche stammered. Then she blushed.

"Take it home with you," said Rose. "Then you can think of something."

Mr. Coday said that since the school session was over, he could give it to Papa when he came into the drugstore.

"All right," said Blanche softly. She took the album from Rose, ran her hand over the mossy cover, and tucked it under her arm. Now she looked at Rose with shining eyes and smiled. She snuffled up the last of her tears. "I'll take good care of it. I promise."

"Good-bye, Blanche," Rose said.

"Good-bye, Rose," said Blanche.

Rose skipped back to be with Mama and Papa. They were still talking to Professor Kay and some other parents. People were leaving the room and going upstairs for lemonade. Rose tugged Mama's skirt and whispered in her ear, *"Lemonade."*

Mama laughed. "Very well," she said. "But where is your album?"

"I gave it to Blanche. She is going to write something in it. Mr. Coday said he will give it to Papa when he goes to town."

"That's very sweet, Rose," said Mama. "Now I have two reasons to be proud of you tonight. A good winner is a gracious winner."

Blanche did not come upstairs to drink lemonade. Rose did not see her again the rest of the evening. But as she walked home in the dark between Mama and Papa, the lantern throwing its quivery circle of light on the path, Rose remembered Blanche's grateful smile. It made Rose happy to think she could make someone smile.

Rose wondered what Blanche might write in her autograph book. She couldn't wait to see.

Harvest Moon

The first cool breaths of autumn stole into the Ozarks at night, pulling heavy blankets of fog over the hills and hollows. Each day the sun rose strong and golden to chase off the gray dawn.

Rose bounded out of bed each morning, delighted she didn't have to dress for school. While she fed the chickens and poured their warmed water into a pan, she took deep breaths of the spicy autumn air. Everywhere Rose looked there were spiderwebs in the grass, sparkling with dewdrops. Puffy white clouds floated in a deep blue sky.

The leaves of the trees had begun to fade. Rose noticed that many of the leaves had jagged holes and edges where insects had been chewing, and brown spots. It was a sure sign that summer was getting old.

Woolly brown and black caterpillars crawled across the barnyard, looking for a good safe corner to spin a cocoon and rest until spring. You could pick one up and put it facing the other way and it would always turn around and crawl rippling off the way it had been going. The wind could bowl them over and they would right themselves and march off in the same direction.

Rose even tried shaking one up in her hand. It curled up into a tiny round pincushion. She carried it to another part of the barnyard. When she set it down, it uncurled itself and started crawling in the very same direction it had been going before. How did it know?

But there was no time for play. This was the month of the harvest moon. They must hurry to gather in the crops before frost.

Mama said they should pick the potatoes

first. "They could wait, but the market is high now. Two and a half cents a pound! And this Ozark weather is almost too good to believe," she said, bent over and huffing as she dug with her hands. She brushed the dirt off a large one and weighed it in her hand. "Two potato crops in one summer! We'll have almost a wagonload to sell and enough to winter over. And we have second plantings of turnips and carrots, yet."

Harvesting potatoes was a treasure hunt. Papa walked along the rows with the shovel and loosened up the hardened hills of earth. Then Rose dug with her hands into the loose soil until she found the pale yellow potatoes clinging to the roots. She made sure to get every one, even the tiniest buttons. They would keep the smallest for eating and trade the big ones at Reynolds' Store.

They stacked the potatoes in piles between the rows. Mama separated the good ones out to sell. When they were done, she and Rose put the graded potatoes into sacks. Then Papa loaded the heavy sacks onto the wagon and drove into town. Rose and Mama stood outside and watched him go. Rose swelled with pride to see the food she had helped grow going off to market.

That night after supper Papa went to the mantel and got down a little book he often wrote in. He sat by the fireplace and scribbled some numbers in pencil. Papa called it his accounts book. He wrote down everything they bought, traded, and sold.

"Why?" asked Rose.

"Any farmer worth his salt keeps his records," said Papa. "It tells how we're doing. See here," he said, showing her the page he was writing on. It had blue lines printed on it, and three columns. The first column had writing, "375 lbs potatoes @ 2 ½¢." In the second column he had written a number, $9.38. The third column was blank.

The book was pages and pages of writing and numbers.

"Every time we trade at Reynolds', I write that down in the third column," Papa explained. "That's a minus. Every time I sell a load of stove wood, or fence rails, or railroad ties I made, or potatoes, or Mama sends in eggs, I write it down in the second column. That is a plus.

"When it comes settling-up time, after the harvest is all in, I will add all the minuses and all the pluses and I can see which one is greater."

"What does it say now?" Rose asked. "Are we plus or minus?"

Papa laughed. "Too soon to say for sure, Rose. But we're getting by."

Papa's account book was a little confusing, but Rose understood that it was very important.

Next Papa dug a shallow pit in the ground in a little clearing between two trees, close to the house. He began to line it with small stones.

"Why, Papa?" Rose wanted to know. "What's it for?"

"Curiosity killed the cat," Papa said. "Run and fetch some straw from the barn."

Rose made several trips, gathering up as much straw as she could carry in her arms. Papa spread the straw over the stones until they were all covered.

He drove the wagon up to the pit. It was piled with the keeping potatoes and the keeping onions that had been hanging from rafters in the barn to dry.

"Now you can help me put all this treasure into the pit," he said.

Papa used the shovel and Rose carried as many as she could in her hands.

"Don't take too many," Papa said. "They mustn't be dropped or bruised. One bad potato will spoil all the rest."

They kept piling up potatoes and onions until Papa said the mound was high enough. Then he sent Rose to fetch more straw. He spread a thick layer of it on top, and shoveled a thick layer of soil on top of that.

The pit had grown into a small hill. Papa dug a hole, just big enough to stick an arm through, on each side. He stuck his hand in to make sure he could reach the potatoes and onions. Then he covered up the holes with some stones and straw. He laid some boards on top of the mound, to make it harder for raccoons and other animals to dig into it and steal the food.

Finally, he stood up and brushed the dirt from his hands.

"All tucked in for winter," he said. "The soil and straw will save them from rot and frost, almost until spring. Anytime we want potatoes or onions, all we have to do is stick an arm in and pluck them out."

The rest of the potatoes and onions went into sacks that Mama stored under the kitchen, through the trapdoor in the floor.

Then they dug up the sweet potatoes that Papa had planted in a corner of the corn patch. They brushed off the dirt and set the gnarled roots out on planks to dry in the sunshine. Rose sorted out the long stringy ones that weren't good for eating. Mama would save them to use for seed next spring.

When the sweet potatoes were dry, Rose and Mama wrapped each one in a scrap of old newspaper. Then they put all the wrapped potatoes in a wooden box in a corner of the kitchen.

They gathered chestnuts that had fallen

from a chestnut tree near the orchard. Mama packed them in layers of salt in a big pickling jar. She tucked the jar away in one of the trunks where they wouldn't be tempted to eat them. She was saving them for Christmas.

One night at supper, after Papa had been to town to pick up some liniment for his sore shoulder, he laid Rose's autograph album on the table. Rose opened it at once and looked on the first page. Blanche had written something there in blue ink. Mama peered over Rose's shoulder and read:

> *Too wise you are, too wise you be;*
> *I see you are too wise for me.*
> *Your friend, Blanche Coday. October 3, 1895.*

Rose tingled with excitement when she read the words "Your friend."

"That's very sweet," said Mama. "I suspect your book will fill up quickly when you go back to school in December."

"I want you and Papa to write something, too," Rose said.

When the dishes had been cleared, Papa took Mama's pen, twisted his mustache for a few minutes, and then scratched away at the page. Rose fidgeted impatiently. Then Papa carefully blotted the page with Mama's blotter and showed it to Rose.

> *To my prairie Rose:*
> *Be faithful in all things,*
> *Superficial in none,*
> *And always remember,*
> *that home is home.*
> *—Papa.*

Mama said she must think of what to write. The next Sunday she spent a long time writing in Rose's book. When she was done she showed it to Rose. It was a poem Mama had composed.

> *There were some naughty flowers once,*
> *Who were careless in their play;*
> *They got their petals torn and soiled*
> *As they swung in the dust all day.*

They went to bed at four o'clock,
With faces covered tight,
To keep the fairy, Drop O'Dew,
From washing them at night.

Poor Drop O'Dew! What could she do?
She said to the Fairy Queen,
"I cannot get those Four o'Clocks
To keep their faces clean."

The mighty Storm King heard the tale;
"My winds and rain," roared he,
"Shall wash those naughty flowers well,
As flowers ought to be."

So raindrops came and caught them all
Before they went to bed,
And washed those little Four o'Clocks
At three o'clock instead.

Mama's poem was beautiful, as good as any in Rose's *McGuffey's Reader.* She read it over and over again, and liked it better each time.

Beans were the next crop to harvest. Abe

and Swiney came to help. They would get a share of the harvest for helping.

For days and days, from morning to night, they picked bean pods off the vines that had climbed up the cornstalks. Rose and Swiney picked the pods that were closest to the ground. Mama and Papa and Abe picked up high.

They all wore tow sacks tied around their waists with string. The tow sacks were long and narrow. Rose's drooped on the ground, and she kept tripping over it. When it began to get full, it was very heavy to drag.

Picking beans was hard work. But Abe made it fun by teaching them a song. They all sang it as they picked, their voices rising from different places in the field.

> "*My papa came from town last night*
> *As sad as a man could be,*
> *His wagon empty, cotton gone,*
> *And not a dime had he.*

"Huzzah! Huzzah!
'Tis strange, Ma did declare!
We make the clothes for all the world,
But few have we to wear."

One morning before the first rooster crow, Rose woke up with a start. A sound had disturbed her sleep, but she didn't know what it was. The soft, slow sighs of Mama and Papa sleeping came from their bed in the corner. A square of bright moonlight from the window lay on the floor at the foot of her bed. The wind was still and the woods quiet, as if they were listening, too.

Rose heard water dripping outside, like rain. But it couldn't be raining if there was moonlight. It was so bright inside that Rose could read the clock face. It was three o'clock.

Then Rose heard the sound again. At first she thought it was a train whistle. It was a wild howling, far away. Then more howling and baying, in different voices. Rose had never heard wolves crying before, but she thought for sure that was what it must be.

She crept out of bed and tiptoed across the cold floor into the kitchen. Fido got up from his sleeping place by the stove and stretched with a tiny moan. Then he tapped across the floor and stood at Rose's feet.

Far away the voices howled again. It was a wild sound that sent shivers up her back. She opened the shutters of one of the windows and looked out. The cool night air flowed over her skin like water.

The whole world was bathed in the bright light of the harvest moon. Heavy dew dripped from all the trees. It gently splattered on the leaves. Moonrays fell like dark sunlight, dappling the ground with shadows. Down toward Fry Creek, fingers of morning mist were starting to creep up among the trees.

Far away the howling took up again. One of the horses snorted in her stall in the barn. The spring purled quietly in the gully behind the house.

Rose went to the front door and opened it. It complained with a tiny squeak. She stepped out onto the porch and looked up at the moon through an opening in the trees. The bright circle of light was clothed in a fuzzy halo that was brownish around the edge.

Rose looked at the moon for the longest time, trying to see the man's face. But it was a harvest moon, when the moon is so bright farmers can work into the night gathering the crops. It was too bright to see the dark spots of its eyes and nose. She had to look away.

She sat down on the porch and stared hard at the trees. She thought she could see the green in the leaves, but only just barely, and only just the darkest green. But even then she wasn't sure. She could just barely see the brown of the soil and rocks. The shadows seemed as crisp as daylight, but the harder she looked the more they were smoothed and softened, the way moss softens a rock. Her eyes kept playing tricks on her.

The gathering mist made the air glow in places. She could see the dark outlines of spiders asleep in their webs in the eaves of the porch, waiting for the earth to warm up and send them a morning meal. Rose felt herself part of the night.

A creaking floorboard in the kitchen startled her. Mama appeared in the doorway, ghostly white in her nightgown.

"Is something the matter?" she asked sleepily. "I heard the door creak."

"Something was howling in the woods," said Rose. "I thought it was wolves."

"I heard it, too," said Mama, sitting down next to Rose on the porch's edge. She yawned. "But it isn't wolves. I think it is just some farmer out hunting a raccoon with his hounds."

They sat in silence for a moment. Rose shivered against the cool morning air. Mama put her arm around Rose's shoulder and squeezed. Then the ghostly shape of Blackfoot came padding toward them across the yard from the barn where he had been sleeping. He mewed softly and rubbed against their legs, purring loudly in the stillness.

"The moonlight is lovely, isn't it?" said Mama. "It's as though you were inside a dream. You can see everything, but you can't see it either."

Rose sat cuddled up against Mama for the longest time, watching the mist floating quietly into the moon-washed yard. She wished that moment could go on forever.

But just then the rooster crowed. A new day was about to begin.